D1510964

BOOKS BY BARBARA CORCORAN

A Dance to Still Music
The Long Journey
Meet Me at Tamerlaine's Tomb
A Row of Tigers
Sasha, My Friend
A Trick of Light
The Winds of Time
All the Summer Voices
The Clown
Don't Slam the Door When You Go
Sam
This Is a Recording
Axe-Time, Sword-Time
Cabin in the Sky
The Faraway Island
Make No Sound
Hey, That's My Soul You're Stomping On
"Me and You and a Dog Named Blue"
Rising Damp
You're Allegro Dead

A Watery Grave

A Watery Grave

by Barbara Corcoran

Atheneum 1983 *New York*

LIBRARY OF CONGRESS CATALOGING IN PUBLICATION DATA

Corcoran, Barbara
A watery grave.

SUMMARY: *Kim and Stella work to find the killer*
when a murder occurs in a household they are visiting.
1. Mystery and detective stories   I. Title
PZ7.C814Wat   1982   [Fic]   82-1726
ISBN   0-689-30919-8   AACR2

Copyright © 1982 by Barbara Corcoran
Published simultaneously in Canada by
McClelland & Stewart, Ltd.
Composition by
American Book-Stratford Graphics, Brattleboro, Vermont
Printed and bound by
Fairfield Graphics, Fairfield, New Jersey
Designed by Mary M. Ahern
First Printing July 1982
Second Printing June 1983

TO

David Tuck

A Watery Grave

1

———

KIM AND STELLA LEANED ON THE HANDLEBARS OF
their bikes and watched the man building the high
wall around the Parris place. It was nearly a year
since their friends the Parrises had sold the house and
moved out of state, but the new owners were just
now taking occupancy. Expressing her disapproval,
Kim pulled down the white duck hat that said CAMP
ALLEGRO around the crown, until it was jammed
down almost to her eyes. She was scowling, and she
pulled back her short dark hair with a gesture so
fierce that it made her wince. Stella, a head taller
than her friend, and as blonde as Kim was dark, put
on the dark glasses that always made her feel invisible.

"I saw Mr. Farley in the paper store," Stella said.
"That's their name, Farley. He was buying the *Globe*
and a *New Yorker*."

"Oh, one of those," Kim said.

"Those what?"

"*New Yorker* types. Sophisticated. City people."

"My Aunt Joan reads the *New Yorker*, and she lives in Vermont in a town of three thousand. You're always classifying people."

Kim rode her bike in a tight circle, just for something to do, and executed a skillful wheelie. "It was Barry Parris that taught me to play tennis, right on that court." She pointed toward a tennis court and a swimming pool, empty of water, still visible through a gap in the unfinished wall.

"But you can't blame the Farleys because the Parrises moved away. They probably don't even know them."

"There you go, always sticking up for everybody. What'd he look like anyway?"

"Mr. Farley? Well, he's about five-ten, a little bit fattish, the way they get when they're middle-aged . . ."

"My dad isn't fattish."

"Well, neither is mine, but we're lucky. Anyway, I knew he was Mr. Farley because his license plate says FARLEY."

"You have to pay extra for that."

"I know. Dr. Endicott says they're loaded."

"He knows them?"

"A classmate of his was their doctor when they

lived wherever they lived, New York state some-where."

"What else did he say?"

"They have some kids. A girl about sixteen that goes to boarding school. A boy around nine or ten."

"They can't have much sense in that family if they hired Georgie Foss to work for them," Kim said, frowning at the man building the wall. "What's the wall for anyway? This isn't exactly a high crime neighborhood."

On the tree-shaded dirt road there was only one other house visible, quite far down the curve. The road looped in a long oval, swinging around when it reached the river and rejoining the main road a mile further down. Across from the Farleys' a dense stand of piney woods smelled good in the late June sun-shine.

"Did you get any decent tennis this morning?" Stella asked. Kim was one of the top players in the county, in her age group. She got up early every morning for a couple of hours of practice.

"Had to wait forever for a court. I wish my dad would join the country club."

The man working on the wall paused and mopped his face with his sleeve. He gave them a foolish grin. "You kids plannin' on sneakin' a swim in the pool?" He gestured toward the swimming pool just visible from where they stood.

"No," Kim said shortly. Georgie Foss was too dumb to bother with.

"Well, if you girls are plannin' on a dip in that pool, I'd advise mighty strong against it." He stood with his trowel in his hand, hoping they'd take the bait.

"Why?" Kim said.

Under her breath Stella said, "Oh, Kim. Ignore him. He's so stupid."

" 'Cause," he said triumphantly, "there ain't no water in 'er." He laughed long and loud, as if the joke were somehow on them.

Stella got on her bike and rode down toward the river. People like Georgie made her uncomfortable. He always looked at her as if she didn't have any clothes on. He was "just a mite backward," Dr. Endicott said, "no harm in him." But she was not so sure of that. Aloud she said, "The world is full of disasters waiting to happen."

"What does that mean?" Kim, following Stella, jerked up on her handlebars and neatly sailed over the root of a big weeping willow.

"People like George Foss. Everybody always thinks they won't do anything bad. Just a little touched in the head, they say, harmless."

"Oh, well, Georgie's no threat." Kim said. "What kind of car does this Farley person have?"

"It's a Bentley."

"Oh, my gosh. They really must be rich. But who cares. We'll never get to know them anyway, if the kids don't go to school here."

"Let's go to the Dairy Queen."

"Okay."

They rode in silence for a few minutes, around the loop, across the state road, past several attractive houses—including Stella's. Then they passed the more modest houses clustered around the village green or on dirt roads that led off the green.

It was a typical New England scene, with the white-steepled Congregational church at one end of the green, the Federal-style town hall at the other. In the center of the green there were beds of roses and a statue of a Revolutionary soldier. Near the statue were brass plaques listing heroes of the various wars, from Revolutionary through Vietnam. Both Kim and Stella had their family names on the memorial plaques, Kim's dating from the Civil War, Stella's from the Spanish-American War. For generations the families in this small town had known each other, but in the last thirty or forty years the charms of the place had been discovered as a place to live by strangers who wanted to escape the city. The newcomers, as they were still called, took care to be on friendly terms with the old-timers, but there was a gulf between new and old that was evident in life-styles, politics sometimes, attitudes toward life. Stella's and Kim's families were among those who, to some extent, bridged the gap. Their fathers worked in Boston and commuted on the 8:35, their mothers did volunteer work at the hospital, sought funds for restoring old buildings, fought for the environment, just as many of the new-comers did, but their roots were "old town." Enough so that Kim and Stella resented a little the incoming Farleys, who were not only totally new but replaced beloved old friends.

"Anyway," Kim said, wrapping her tongue around her triple strawberry cone, "I'd like a chance to use that tennis court now and then, when the town courts are full."

"My mother says. . . ."

Both girls turned to look at the speaker. It was Nicole, whose family had been around a few years, but who was not really a friend. The problem was, they had decided long before, that she tried too hard.

"My mother says there's some kind of big mystery."

Stella didn't feel like hearing what Nicole's bumptious mother had to say about anything, but Kim was curious. "What kind of mystery?"

Nicole rolled her eyes and ordered a banana split "with everything, don't forget the whipped cream." When she answered Kim, it was in her usual maddening tone, suggesting that she knew the answer but her lips were sealed. "If it were spread all over town, it wouldn't be a mystery, would it?"

(8)

"That means you don't know," Kim said.

"It does not. It means I'm not going to repeat my confidential knowledge."

"Does your mother know these people?" Stella asked, less interested in the answer than in averting a Kim–Nicole argument, which could go on for hours.

"My father used to do business with Mr. Farley, when we lived in Scarsdale."

"Oh." The reminder that Nicole had once had a father, always stopped Stella cold. It was just too hard to imagine. From scraps of conversation heard at home, she gathered that the man had "flown the coop," as her father inelegantly put it, years ago. She wondered if Nicole remembered him. She hardly ever spoke of him, and then only in the context of something her mother had said. Nicole's mother was a large, loud, and imposing woman, and even Stella's friendly and tolerant mom found her a bit hard to take.

"What kind of business is this Mr. Farley in?" Kim asked.

"He was on Wall Street, but he's retired now. Something to do . . ." Nicole paused and inhaled a mouthful of whipped cream. ". . . with the mystery, because actually he's not all that old."

"Probably a crook," Kim said. "He was probably drummed out of Wall Street."

"No, it's more like a tragedy," Nicole said. "A

(9)

great personal tragedy." She looked at them with dark, tragedy-laden eyes. And then in a flash that expression faded, and she was smug, patronizing Nicole again. "You can play tennis with me at the club, Kim."

Kim tried not to show her annoyance. Her own family had never belonged to the club, and it irked her that Nicole, who hardly knew one end of a racket from the other, had access to those good courts when she did not. "Oh, thanks," she said, "but I'm going to have a frightfully busy summer."

"Doing what?"

"I have a number of projects." Kim threw the bottom of her cone into the trash can and prepared to ride off. Not since the day she had found a dead fly in the bottom of her ice cream cone had she eaten one right down to the end. "Coming, Stell? See you, Nicole."

"I wish we were going back to camp," Stella said, as they pedaled down the road. "Don't you?"

"Yes, but I'd rather wait till things get straightened out. Maybe next summer we can."

The summer camp they had enjoyed so much the year before had been leased to someone else while their director recovered from a near-fatal car accident.

"Hey, look," Stella said, "that's your mom's car in my driveway. Want to come in?"

"Sure. Maybe I can shake her down for money for the show tonight. My allowance is in parlous shape. She hates to say no in front of other people."

The girls swooped into the semi-circular drive, their tires crunching on the gravel. They left their bikes sprawled on the grass near Kim's mother's yellow Honda and went in the blue front door.

The mothers were in the living room drinking tea, and they looked excited.

"Can we come in?" Stella asked. She threw her blue cotton sweater onto the hall bench.

Both mothers turned to smile at them.

"Of course you can. Would you like tea?"

"Coke?" Stella said tentatively. There were frequent family arguments about the amount of caffeine in Coke, the amount of sugar, the effect on the teeth, and other similar topics that usually left Stella wishing she had never brought it up.

"Tea, I think." Her mother had already gone for two more cups, and Stella wondered why she had bothered to ask. Teenagers were asked their opinions on things, but they were not old enough yet for anyone to pay attention to their answers. Maybe next year?

Actually the tea did taste good, and after they had had a few sips, Stella's mother said, "We were discussing an idea we're excited about."

Kim's mother said, "It only just came up, you see, when your father, . . ." She looked at Kim. ". . . when he got that bonus and the time off."

Kim yawned. "What bonus? What time off?"

"Kim, we told you. We've got two glorious weeks—"

Stella's mother finished in a rush of words. "—and we're going on a vacation, to Bermuda!"

Both girls snapped to attention. Stella said, "We *are?*"

The mothers looked at each other, and then Stella's mother said, "Well, not all of us, dear. That is, we can't make it a family affair. The air fares alone are—"

Kim interrupted. "You mean you're going without us?"

"Only for two weeks, honey," her mother said. "You understand."

"The heck I do," Kim said flatly.

Stella, the practical one, said, "But what will happen to us?"

In a dismal voice Kim said, "We'll go bad. We'll sink from evil to evil. In two weeks' time—it doesn't take long, you know, to go right straight to the dregs."

Stella's mother laughed. "Kim, you should go on the stage. You won't have such a bad time of it. We've just talked with your friend Hen, and she's agreed to come and stay with you—"

The girls interrupted with sudden yelps of delight. "Hen! Hen Norton!"

"Your beloved swimming counselor," Stella's mother said. "You see what luck . . ."

"You'll stay here, and everything will be fine," Kim's mother said.

"Wait a minute," Kim said. "Why isn't Hen in summer school? She said she was going."

"She changed her mind. They thought she was going to have her appendix out, but it's quieted down, and the doctors want her to take it easy in July and have the appendectomy in August. So you mustn't make life too strenuous for her. . . ."

The girls were too happy and excited to listen to admonitions. Hen Norton had been their favorite counselor at camp the year before. They would have a wonderful time with Hen.

They ran upstairs to make plans.

"And *don't*," Kim said, "don't tell Nicole."

"Not unless it's absolutely necessary." They shook hands in agreement. The summer was looking better all the time.

2

___

KIM AND STELLA RODE THEIR BIKES DOWN TO THE river, just to see if it was getting any warmer, even though their mothers had said they could not . . . absolutely could not . . . no arguments please! . . . go swimming before July 1.

"What's so sacred about July one anyway?" Kim said, kicking off her green and white striped canvas shoe and testing the water with bare toes. She drew back quickly.

"Cold?" Stella asked.

"Maybe a little bit. But I bet it'll be warm before July one. Maybe Hen can talk them into letting us swim."

Stella trickled her fingers in the water and shook her head. "When my mom says, 'No arguing,' it's hopeless. She never gives in."

They sat on the bank studying the soft, inviting swirl of the river. The sun coming through the leaves above them dappled their heads.

"The what's-er-names filled their pool yesterday," Kim said in a brooding voice.

"Farleys. I know that. Everybody in town knows it because Georgie Foss's no-good brother-in-law got the job, and Georgie's bragging all over town. If the Farleys knew anything at all, they'd never hire Patrick Moon. He's drunk or high on drugs so often, he'll probably fall in and drown himself, first thing."

"And too stupid to get out if he fell in."

They smiled, having satisfactorily demolished Patrick Moon. Kim leaned back on the damp earth and closed her eyes.

After a while Stella said, "A car's coming."

"I suppose you hear it with your supersonic ear."

"Listen. You can hear it, too."

After a moment Kim nodded. "Car coming. Well, that's life in exciting West Haverford. You wait long enough, and a car comes up the road. No wonder so many of the natives die of stroke. It's the pace that gets 'em."

"It's a 1968 T-Bird," Stella said, as the car came into sight.

Kim shook her head. Stella's knowledge of cars always amazed her. It seemed out of character. She was especially good at older, exotic cars, and she knew about races too. She could tell you who won the Indy 500 for all of the last five years.

"In good condition," Stella said, watching the car slow down. The driver had seen her. He was a young man, perhaps in his early twenties, with the kind of look that went with the car. A girl was sitting in the bucket seat next to him. He beckoned to Stella and Kim.

"Ask you a question?" he called.

They looked at each other. "He's not planning kidnap," Kim said. "Car's too small."

They walked slowly to the side of the road and looked at him from a short distance.

"Hi," he said, flashing a broad smile. "My name is Bill. I'm looking for the Farley place. Can you tell me where it is? They moved here just recently, but I *think* it's this road . . ."

"I think we should have gone on to the next left," the girl said, in a slightly argumentative voice. She was very pretty.

"Either way," Stella said. "It's a loop road. The Farleys' place is on your left, quarter of a mile. There's a sign."

"Hey, thanks a whole lot. Very good directions." He looked at the girl. "Aren't those good directions?"

"Superb," she said in a bored voice. "Let's go, Bill, for heaven's sake."

He revved the engine, gave them another smile and a jaunty wave, and the car zoomed down the road, leaving the girls in a cloud of dust.

Kim coughed and wiped her eyes. "A gentleman through and through."

"They forget. When they're in a powerhouse like that, they forget there's anybody outside."

"Well, he was good-looking. Do the Farleys have kids that age?"

"I don't think so. Anyway if it was a Farley, he'd know where he lived."

"Oh, brilliant deduction. I meant it might be friends of a Farley that age."

A thin voice floating on air said, "There's no Farley that age."

Stella and Kim jumped and looked around. No one was there. They stared at each other.

"Listen," Stella said indignantly, "if you've been learning ventriloquism without telling me. . . ."

Kim shook her head wildly. "I swear." Again they looked behind them and up and down the road. "Maybe it was the wind?"

"Sure, only there isn't any wind, and the wind does not pronounce its words that distinctly. I mean that wind could have passed a reading and speaking test at school." She frowned and said in a loud clear voice, "Is someone there?"

There was no reply at first, but just as they were

beginning to look relieved, the voice came again. "Only in spirit," it said.

That made Kim mad. She put her hands on her hips and said severely, "This is not funny. There is no such thing as disembodied spirits speaking English. When voices float down from the trees, there has to be—" She stopped. "Trees!" She looked up into the branches of the oak tree near them, and at that moment a boy jumped lightly to the ground.

He was about ten years old, with a small, tanned face, and fierce blue eyes. He stood just far enough from them so they could not grab him. He did not smile. "What language," he demanded, "would a spirit speak?"

Cross at having been fooled, Kim said, "How do I know? It would depend on where he was from, I suppose. A French spirit would speak French, Hungarian would speak Hungarian. . . . Only there aren't any spirits anyway."

"What if it was a spirit from outer space? It might not even sound like a human voice. It might chirp like a bird. Maybe half the birds you think you hear chirping away are spirits from outer space. Maybe they don't have voices as we know them. I think it's pretty rude not even to listen."

Kim and Stella looked at each other. "He's crazy," Kim said.

"I've never seen you before," Stella said to him.

"Who are you? I mean I know about every kid in this town."

"You don't know me, but here I am. I may be from outer space." With sudden interest he added, "Or maybe *you* are. After all, I never saw you before either."

Stella frowned at him. "Is your name Farley by any chance?"

"It's not by chance at all. My mother is married to my father, and why shouldn't I be called Farley? That's who I am."

"Well," Kim said, "why didn't you say so?"

"You didn't ask me."

"Who was that that just asked for directions?" Kim said. "Not, I guess, that it's any of my business."

"But you're eaten up with curiosity. People are always curious about the Farleys."

"Why?"

He shrugged. "I suppose because we're weird." Without any preliminaries he wheeled around and ran off along the road toward the Farley place.

"Ask a silly question," Kim said, "get a silly answer."

"Dr. Endicott asked my mom to ask Mrs. Farley to the church guild tea."

"A person doesn't have to be asked, do they?"

"No, but he said it would be friendly. He said Mrs. Farley is sort of shy and retiring."

(*19*)

"Well, I can't say as much for her son. That kid scared the heck out of me."

"Me too. I mean, voices in the air."

They got on their bikes and started back to the village, taking the long way around in order to pass the Farley place. The white T-Bird was partly in view at the end of the gravel drive. When slow Georgie Foss finished the wall, a person wouldn't be able to look in at the house, but now you could still see most of it. It was a very large pale yellow house with white trim, like the houses Samuel McIntire had built for the sea captains in Salem. They could see Mr. Truitt's bald head as he struggled with a newly painted windowbox of geraniums. A woman came out onto the porch and spoke to Mr. Truitt, but she was too far away to be seen clearly.

"Who cleans house, I wonder?" Kim said. "That's a big place."

"She brought someone from New York."

They had nearly passed the driveway when another car came along the road from the opposite direction, an Audi Fox, 1980, as Stella pointed out.

It too had a young man driver with a young woman beside him. He was driving fast, and the girls instinctively speeded up to get out of his way. With a shower of gravel he slewed the car into the Farleys' drive and in a moment was out of their line of vision.

"We're spending the morning eating dust kicked up by the Farleys' friends," Kim said, wiping her face with her arm. "Let's get out of here." She pedaled fast down the road, and a few minutes later they were drinking root beer floats.

Nicole came up behind them. "Hi," she said. "What are you guys up to?"

"Gaining weight, mostly," Kim said.

"Your mother said you rode out to the river."

"My mother speaks the truth."

"How was it?"

"Wet." Kim looked at Nicole. "There's something you're dying to tell us. Okay, what is it?"

Nicole gazed around furtively, giggled, and said, "I've seen her."

"Seen who? My mother? I see her every day. It's no big deal."

"Silly, I don't mean your mother. I mean *her*. The Farley girl."

In spite of themselves they were interested.

"What's she like?" Stella asked.

"Where'd you see her?" Kim asked.

"We-ell," Nicole said prolonging her advantage. "You'll never guess."

"We aren't even trying," Kim said, "so tell us or don't."

"My mother stopped her mother downtown to welcome her to West Haverford. Mrs. Farley didn't really remember my mother, I don't think—I mean, she seems kind of out of it, you know what I mean? But my mother made her remember."

Stella gave Kim a look that said, "I'll bet she did." Nicole's mother was a ruthless woman.

"And she had her daughter with her, and I was with my mother, see, so we all got introduced."

"What's she like?"

"Stuck-up."

"What'd she talk about?"

"Nothing. After she said, 'How do you do,' in a very affected voice, she did not say word one."

Kim chuckled.

It was some time before Nicole finished her account, but all it really amounted to was that Mrs. Farley seemed vague and Jennifer Farley was stuck-up.

When they finally got away from her, Kim said, "So what do we know that we didn't know before? Nothing. In my opinion anyone who doesn't talk to Nicole is showing good sense. And any woman who doesn't remember Nicole's mother—"

Stella finished it for her. "—has never met her."

"If this Jennifer doesn't take to Nicole," Kim said, "by the law of averages she ought to like us. Or is that the second law of thermodynamics. Anyway, you see what it all leads to."

"What?"

"We get invited to use the tennis court."

Stella's eyes brightened. "And the pool!"

"Preferably with water in it." Kim lifted her arm and smashed an imaginary tennis ball over an imaginary net.

"I can feel that cool water now," Stella said.

"We'd better not count our pools before they're splashed." Kim laughed and ducked the slap Stella aimed at her. "Maybe we can take Hen swimming there."

"We haven't even met them yet."

"Think positive." Kim jumped the front wheel of her bike over a curb onto the sidewalk. "It may turn into a good summer after all."

3

STELLA SAT ON THE SUITCASE THAT HER MOTHER WAS
trying to close.

"Your father's right," her mother said. "We need
new luggage."

Kim was sitting cross-legged on the floor bouncing
a red tennis ball. "Vuitton, that's the stuff to get."

"If we bought Vuitton, we wouldn't have enough
money left to travel."

"That guy that's visiting the Farleys, the one with
the T-Bird, he had snazzy luggage. Or else his girl
did."

Stella's mother bit her lip. "I almost forgot. I told
Mrs. Farley I'd send her my copy of *The Remembrancer.*"

"Why?" Stella asked.

"Oh, I took her to the guild tea, you know, and

Father Pollard put a little piece in *The Remembrancer* about the guests who came to the tea."

Kim looked amused. "You mean this woman, this woman with swimming pools and tennis courts and people in T-Birds wants an extra copy of our church paper, circulation four hundred and two on a good week, just because it had her name in it?"

Stella's mother looked vaguely troubled. "Don't laugh at her, Kim dear. She's really very sweet, and awfully—I don't know—shy, withdrawn. I think she feels insecure for some reason."

Kim shook her head. "Hard to picture."

"We humans do not live by tennis courts alone," Stella said. "Anyway, Mom, we'll take her *The Remembrancer*." She shot a significant look at Kim, whose face immediately lit up.

"She'll be charmed with us and invite us to use the court and the pool," Kim said. "Stell, you're a genius."

"Now look," Stella's mother said, "if you're going to be conniving about it, I'll just mail it to her."

"No, Mom, let us take it. We ought to welcome the Farley girl to the neighborhood anyway."

Her mother did not look convinced of the purity of Stella's motives, but she ignored it all and went on. "I've left a list for Hen," she said. She looked at her watch. "Your father ought to be at Logan about now.

That means they'll be here in . . . maybe an hour—"

"Give or take for traffic," Kim said. "Gosh, won't it be good to see old Hen!"

"I've left her the phone number and of course address of our hotel, and Dr. Endicott's number just in case anything, God forbid, should happen. Your mother has a list for her too, Kim. Don't forget to give it to her. Remind her that Monday and Thursday are trash collection days. The relatives all know we'll be gone, so they won't be writing. If Grandma calls, reassure her. She seems to think Hen is a child, too."

"Hen is terribly responsible," Kim said.

"I know that, or I wouldn't be leaving you. Now, why don't the two of you run along for a while? I'd like a quick nap before your father and Hen get here. I swear, I'm almost too tired to take this trip." She flopped onto her bed and closed her eyes.

As she left the room, Stella picked up the little, mimeographed, church newsletter, *The Remembrancer*. When they were outside, she said, "Let's take it over now."

Kim didn't need to say "Take what, where?" "Sure," she said, and went to get her bike.

"Nicole says her mother put up the Farleys' name for membership at the club," Kim said.

"Why do they need the club? They've got everything."

"Why do they need Nicole's mother? And why is Nicole's mother so kind and charitable to them? She never even speaks to most of the people in this town."

"Because the Farleys are loaded," said Kim. "Don't tell me you can't fathom the noisome depths of Nicole's mother's revolting psyche!" She turned into the Farleys' driveway and cast a covetous look at the tennis court as they passed it. The two young men they had seen before were playing singles, and one of the girls sat on the wrought iron bench beside the court, watching the ball with the metronome motion of the head that people fall into at a tennis match.

"The T-Bird guy isn't too bad," Kim murmured. "The other one has a weak backhand."

"Bill," Stella said. "The T-Bird is named Bill."

"Well, William just served a bummer. He knows we're watching. He's a show-off." She turned away and pedaled fast up to the front of the house.

Even though the Parrises had been gone only a year, the house seemed as if it had never sheltered them. The changes were small and subtle, but they were many. The windowboxes, for one thing. They brightened the rather somber facade, but they also robbed it of some of its dignity, a big neo-classical mansion trying to look like a Cape Cod cottage. They should have planted flowerbeds next to the house, Stella thought, in the ground, between the arbor vitae and the mugho pine.

And the windows looked different. The Farleys had had Levelors installed. Kim's house had Levelors in the downstairs rooms, and Stella liked them there, but here they looked out of place. Why am I being so critical, she wondered, and knew the answer at once: she missed the Parrises, and resented the newcomers. She imagined her father's voice saying, "Hardly fair, old girl, is it?" He was a great believer in looking at both sides.

She hesitated, with her hand on the big brass knocker. It was new too, a lion's head with a ring in its mouth, like the famous knocker at 10 Downing Street. Kim bypassed her and pushed the doorbell. They could hear the musical chime in the hall inside.

It occurred to Stella that a maid might come to the door and just take *The Remembrancer* for Mrs. Farley, and they would have accomplished nothing by coming over here. She had hoped that they might have at least a glimpse of the Farleys, one or all.

The door was flung open so abruptly that Stella jerked backward and stepped on Kim's sandaled foot. Kim stifled an "Ouch!" The person in the doorway was their acquaintance, the Farley boy.

With no greeting he said, in a voice unusually deep and resonant for a child, "Do you know anything about Stonehenge?"

The two girls looked at each other, mystified.

"Personally?" Kim said.

"Besides what everybody knows or thinks they know, I mean. Don't give me that Druid garbage. What about the other stones? And that ditch. . . ." He got a faraway, puzzled look, as if he saw something in the distance.

A girl appeared behind him in the hall. "David, what are you doing?" she said. "Go on, beat it." She gave him a little shove. He shrugged.

"You never know till you ask," he said, and went back to the Parrises' den, where a radio voice was speaking with a British accent. Stella recognized it as the BBC Science Program.

"Don't mind him," the girl said. "He's crazy." She was slim, with dark hair, and large gray eyes flecked with gold, eyes as expressionless as stone. She looked at them and waited.

"We . . . uh. . . ." Stella said. "Are you the . . . I mean. . . ." She tried to think what the Avon lady always said. "Are you the young lady of the house?"

A flicker of amusement crossed the girl's face. "You could say that. Are you selling Girl Scout cookies or something?"

"No, no," Stella said. For some reason this girl rattled her. Maybe it was her poise; she was so darned cool. "My mother promised to send your mother . . . uh . . . this." She thrust *The Remembrancer* toward the girl, who took a startled step backward.

Another voice came from a room off the hall. "Jennifer? Is someone there?" A woman came into view. She was the kind of woman that one didn't see too often in West Haverford, where women paid their obligatory weekly visits to the beauty parlor but came out looking well-groomed rather than spectacular. This woman came closer to spectacular. She was too thin, as if she had dieted strenuously and lost weight too fast; she had the deep, lacquered tan one gets from a sunlamp; her hair was just a bit too blonde for West Haverford, and her makeup a bit too obvious. She looked, Stella decided, "New York, suburban."

By contrast her voice was soft and her accent Southern, and as she came toward them, her manner was diffident. Stella remembered her mother's trying to find the word for her: shy, withdrawn, insecure. She did seem all of those things, as she smiled uncertainly at them.

"Some kids have something or other for you," Jennifer said, and turned away.

Stella wanted to say, "Wait, wait. Let's get to know each other," but she addressed herself politely to Mrs. Farley. "My mother said she promised you a copy of the church newsletter. We brought it over." She held it out.

Mrs. Farley's face flushed with pleasure. "Why,

how nice of her to remember. And how nice of you to bring it. Please come in."

"Oh, that's all right," Stella said. "We just—"

"No, please. You must let me get you a cool drink. Do you like that orange drink that comes in cans? The children like that. Sunkist, is it?" She fluttered her hands, as if she were shooing chickens. "Come in here where it's sunny. I don't know where Jennifer disappeared to. . . ." She looked around vaguely.

"We really can't stay. . . ." Stella was saying, but Kim gave her a jab with her elbow, and they followed Mrs. Farley into what had been the Parrises' library. It looked like another room altogether. There were almost no books, except for some science fiction paperbacks. Most of the shelves held ceramic figurines, a collection of Bilson-Battersea enamelled boxes, a collection of salt and pepper shakers, mostly of the souvenir variety: "Souvenir of Atlantic City," "Souvenir of San Diego." And a collection of silver bowling trophies. On one wall the shelves had been removed to make room for an elk head, whose glassy eyes stared at them from a great philosophical distance.

The two girls sat on the wicker loveseat, not quite sure whether it was all right to put their feet on the white sheepskin rug.

Then Stella could hardly believe her ears as Kim

said, "Rooms certainly change, don't they. I mean with different people."

Mrs. Farley looked blank for a moment, almost as if she had dozed off. Then she said, "Oh, you knew the Parrises?"

"They were our best friends." Kim sounded stern.

"Well, I hope you will be our friends, too." Mrs. Farley smiled hopefully. "Do you like to swim? Do you play tennis?"

Kim brightened. "Both."

"Then do come. Please. Any time." She frowned anxiously. "Though you'd better call first. Sometimes we. . . . At the moment we have house guests. But any time they aren't. . . ." She broke off almost all of her sentences. Then as if with an effort she said, "Come Saturday. Yes, come Saturday at two o'clock. Please do."

"We'd love to," Kim said.

For a moment they all sat there, smiling uncertainly. Then Stella stood up. "We'd better push off, Mrs. Farley. My folks are leaving for Bermuda tomorrow, and they've got a lot for me to do."

"Oh, I remember now. She told me. The Princess Hotel. Lovely. I wish I were going, too." She suddenly looked as if she might burst into tears.

The girls rode their bikes fast up the driveway to the road, scattering gravel behind them. Not until they had passed the length of the Farley wall did either of them speak.

Then Kim said, "Thanks a million for the lovely cool nonexistent orange drink, Mrs. Farley. I really dig that Sunkist, man."

Riding no hands, Stella turned to look at her friend. "Oh, Kim," she said, "that lady's got problems."

4

IT SEEMED AS THOUGH THEY HAD NOT STOPPED TALKING since Hen arrived. They had not seen her since the previous summer, when she was the swimming counselor at their camp, although they had written often. Hen had one more year of pre-med, and she had been working hard all year. The girls thought she looked tired and pale, but they said so only to each other.

"We'll give her a real easy time," Kim said. "No problems."

"She asked me about Dr. Endicott," Stella said. "Like is he any good. I think she worries about that darned appendix."

"Well, she's having it out next month. We'll build her up while she's here. Listen, you make some of those super bramble things that you make, and I'll make fudge. That'll fatten her up."

Stella rolled her eyes. "It'll fatten *me* up too."

But on Friday afternoon they insisted that Hen take a nap, while they functioned busily in the kitchen.

"You're treating me like your old maiden aunt," Hen protested, laughing.

"You're suffering from jet lag," Kim said. "You've got to rest."

"Jet lag from New York to Boston?" But Hen looked glad, in spite of what she said, for the chance to lie down.

When she came downstairs again, there were two pans of marshmallow fudge and a cooling rack stacked with brambles. Kim was making banana milkshakes in the blender.

"And you cleaned up the kitchen!" Hen said. "What good kids. Oh, I do feel a lot better." She bit through the warm crust of a bramble into raisins and nuts and mincemeat. "I never had one of these. They're good." Her face took on a look of pleased surprise. "Why, they're terrific!"

Pleased, Stella said, "Eat some of Kim's fudge, too. It's full of vitamins and minerals. Listen, Hen, we haven't told you about the swimming party. We're invited to swim in a pool tomorrow afternoon. A terrific pool, at a private house. You're going to love it."

"Am I invited?"

"We're invited en masse," Kim said hastily. She and Stella had agreed that of course Mrs. Farley wouldn't mind their bringing Hen. Probably wouldn't even notice.

When the time came, two o'clock on Saturday afternoon, Stella did feel a little nervous. She hoped they weren't being rude, bringing along an extra person.

Hen parked Stella's father's Mazda between the tennis court and the pool. No one was in sight. They had worn their swimsuits under their shorts and shirts, but there were a couple of tents that had appeared since they were here before, tipi-shaped affairs in vivid Roman striped canvas, which apparently served as dressing rooms. Off beyond the tennis court was the guest house that the oldest Parris boy had lived in after he grew into independence.

Feeling a bit uneasy, the three of them sat down beside the pool, taking off their shorts and blouses and testing the water with their toes.

"Nice pool," Hen said. "Good diving board."

It was an Olympic-sized pool with a shallow end, and at the opposite end a new-looking board. The canvas cushions from the poolside chairs had been stacked up in a corner. The pool sparkled, as if it had been recently cleaned.

"I wonder where everybody is," Stella said. "Do you think I should go up to the house and say we're here?"

"Nah," Kim said. "Probably she asked us on pur-

pose for a day when the company wouldn't be here."
She tucked her straight dark hair behind her ears.

"Well, if you don't think we'll get driven off with
a shotgun," Hen said, "I'm for making hay while the
sun shines." She stood up, poised a moment on the
edge of the pool, up on her toes with her arms ex-
tended, and then dived in.

"I wish I could dive like that," Stella said.

"Me too." Kim dived in, not with Hen's style but
well enough.

Stella stood up. That first plunge was always hard
to make. "All right," she said, "here goes nothing."
She jumped in, feet-first, making a great splash. Hen
ducked the avalanche of water and made a face.

"Who's your swimming instructor?" she called to
Stella.

Laughing, Stella pointed at her. "Your fault."

For a few minutes they swam the length of the
pool, back and forth, passing each other, enjoying the
cool, silky feeling of the water.

Stella, first one to climb the steel ladder, was the
first to see the boy, David Farley. He was sitting on
the grass that began just beyond the cement surround.
He was wearing a pair of dingy white shorts and a
peaked black cap that said CAT, and he was chewing
on a piece of grass.

"Hi," Stella said. "You startled me."

When he didn't answer, she said, "Your mother

(37)

asked us to come over and swim today."

"I know."

"Is she in the house?"

"She's lying down. Not to be disturbed. She's got a migraine."

"Oh, I'm terribly sorry. Do you think we'll disturb her or anything?"

He shook his head.

Stella sat down beside him.

"That country doctor gave her a pill big enough to choke a horse. She'll be zonked out."

Stella considered the situation, and when Kim climbed out, she repeated it to her. "David," Stella said, "do you think it's okay for us to be here?"

He shrugged. "Everybody has to be somewhere." He stared at Hen as Stella introduced them. "Do you know anything about Stonehenge?" he asked her.

"Not really. Are you interested in Stonehenge?"

"I'm making a model of it. Some things I'm not sure of."

"I guess there are some things even the scientists aren't sure of."

He studied her. "I was there when they built it."

"Really?" Hen managed to sound politely interested. "That must have been fascinating."

He banged the flat of his hand on the ground. "But I can't remember everything. Memory of details can really get screwed up in the reincarnation process. All you remember are *impressions*."

After a moment Hen said, "Maybe it'll come to you."

"They've promised to take me there next year, but they won't. They didn't last year. It would be only as a tourist anyway. I couldn't get near enough to find out anything. You know why? Because people stole chips off the rocks. Can you believe it?"

Stella looked at Kim. She was amazed not so much at what he was saying as that he was talking so much to Hen. With them he had not been communicative. Kim shrugged and went back to the pool. Why waste precious time? She went off the board in a neat swan, and Stella felt a pang of envy.

She wandered off on the warm, freshly cut grass, trying to remember whether you could see the river from here. She passed the tennis court, whose net hung limp, and came upon the pretty little gray-shingled guest house with its blue shutters. She and Kim and the younger Parris kids used to use it sometimes as a hideaway. That was before Ben took it over. She wondered if young David liked it.

Without thinking that it might not be the thing to do, she stopped at one of the windows and peered in, more than half expecting it to look the way it had when she played there. But like the big house, it had been completely redone. In place of the old bunks, there were twin beds with maple headboards and white "popcorn" spreads, with seven or eight brightly colored small pillows on each bed. There was a new tile-top round table with two chairs. The bookcase was gone, and on the walls there were flower prints. The door to the small bathroom was half-open, and as Stella stood there, it came all the way open and a young woman walked into the main room.

Stella was so startled, she didn't move. Fortunately, the young woman had not seen her. It was the person who had been in the car that day, the T-Bird. She was a very pretty girl, very feminine-looking, with shoulder-length hair and rounded features. At the moment she was crying as if her heart would break. As Stella watched, the girl threw herself down on the thick rug beside one of the beds, buried her head in her arms, and sobbed.

Stella pulled back quickly. What she was doing was terrible, spying on somebody, watching them cry like that. But she hadn't meant to. For a moment she wondered if she should ask the girl if she needed help, but then she thought how upset *she* would be if someone invaded her privacy like that. She went quickly back to the pool.

David was gone. Kim was diving again, and Hen was just surfacing, tossing her wet hair back from her face.

"Hi," she said. "Where'd you go?" And without waiting for an answer, "That David has quite an imagination, hasn't he? The last thing he told me was, 'Somebody around here's going to get killed.' "

Stella stared at her. "Killed!"

Hen laughed. "Anything to get attention." A moment later she grabbed her side, gasped, and said, "Oh, no," in a low voice.

"What is it, Hen? Have you got a pain? Is it your appendix?" For a moment Stella felt very angry with her parents, going off and leaving her with all these responsibilities.

A few seconds later, when she had helped Hen into a deck chair, she saw Jennifer Farley approaching them. Jennifer was wearing riding breeches and an open-necked white shirt and shiny dark brown riding boots. She began to speak as she came up to them. "My mother is sorry not to greet you. She has a headache. She—" She broke off, looking at Hen. "Who's that? Is she sick?"

Quickly Stella explained.

"Dr. Endicott is still at the house talking to my dad about fishing. I'll get him." Jennifer turned and ran toward the big house.

"I feel like a fool," Hen said, and then groaned as another pain caught her.

"Listen, don't worry. What a break Doc Endicott is here. He's almost like our father or something." Stella held Hen's hand tightly.

Dr. Endicott seemed to arrive in no time at all. He

was a short, plump man, but when he moved, he moved fast. He gave Hen a few pokes and asked some questions. "To be on the safe side," he told Stella and Kim, "I'm going to take this young lady into the hospital for a better look at things."

"We'll come with you."

"No." He looked over and recognized the Mazda. "You go home and stay put, so I can find you when I want to talk to you. I'll get someone to drive the car home later. Just walk home and stay put." He patted Stella's shoulder. "And don't worry. It's not a federal case, you know, having an appendix out. Dr. Swayne is still in town, hasn't gone on his vacation yet, and there's nobody better. That is, if we need him."

Looking white, Hen said, "What about the girls? I'm supposed to look after them."

"One step at a time, young lady." He tossed his car keys at Jennifer. "Jennifer, bring my car down here, as close as you can get to the pool without ruining Sandy Truitt's lawn, will you?"

Jennifer ran, and a minute later she backed the car right up to the pool's deck.

"Sandy will faint," Dr. Endicott said. He helped Hen to her feet and got her into the car.

"Mr. Truitt gets paid to fix the lawn," Jennifer said. "So he has a little extra lawn to fix. No big deal." She had not smiled at all. Now she looked directly at Hen and said, "I hope you feel better," and left.

(*42*)

5

STELLA AND KIM SAT HUDDLED NEAR THE PHONE IN Stella's house, but when Dr. Endicott got in touch with them, he came in person. It had been several hours since he had taken Hen to the hospital.

He rang the doorbell and came in without waiting. "There you are, hanging onto the phone looking miserable," he said cheerfully. "Not to worry, girls, not to worry. I caught Dr. Swayne on the third green. Darned good man, Swayne."

"Is she all right?" Kim said. "Is she coming home?"

He sat down and fanned himself with his hand. "Hot out. She won't be home just yet awhile, but she's in good hands. Dr. Swayne will take out that pesky appendix in the morning. She's had a shot and she's snoozing. Worried about you of course, but I told her I'd be responsible for you."

"We'll be all right here," Stella said.

"Well, your folks would want you nearer some grownups just in case. And Mrs. Farley called while I was mulling this over, said she heard about Harriet from her daughter. She insists on your staying in her guest house. It's not exactly under somebody's wing, but there's a phone connected with the house, and who for gracious sakes is going to bother you there? You can swim and play tennis and keep out of mischief."

"We don't have to eat with them, do we?" Kim said.

"Not if you don't want to. Mrs. Farley's apt to forget all about you, to tell you the truth, but I don't see that there's any risk in it. You're not infants."

"One of their house guests is already in the cabin," Stella said.

"Mrs. Farley said something about that, said she moved the girl up to the house." He ran his hand through his thin white hair. "If you run into any problems, give me a call. Now why don't you put a few things in a bag, pajamas, toothbrush, whatever, and I'll drop it off for you. You can ride your bikes over there."

Before they left, Stella called Hen's mother to tell her about the impending operation. Then they spent half an hour trying to decide what flowers to send Hen. Finally they bought triple burgers with fries and milkshakes to go and started off for the guest house at the Farleys'.

The four house guests were sunning beside the pool, the girls lying on big beach towels, the owner of the Audi stretched out on the diving board, and the one called Bill dangling his legs in the pool. He looked up and smiled at them.

"Hi. I remember you. Welcome to Fat City." He turned to one of the girls. "Remember these kids, Anne?"

She murmured a hi into the depths of her bath towel.

"I'm Bill," he said, "that's Anne, that's Alicia, and that corpse stretched out on the diving board is Hank."

Hank lifted his head and said hello. He was dark and good-looking and unsmiling.

"I'm Stella and this is Kim," Stella said. "We're . . . uh . . . going to sleep in the guest house."

"We know," Anne murmured.

Bill stood up, teetered on the edge of the pool, lost his balance and went in feet-first, arms waving. The one named Alicia gave a thin shriek of laughter.

"That's a silly age," Kim said as she and Stella went into the cabin. "Gosh, doesn't it look different?"

There were flowers, and a bowl of chocolate chip cookies. A note beside the cookies said:

Welcome to our happy though chaotic home. I am delighted to be able to repay a fraction of all the kindness your mothers have shown to me. Alas, I am hors du combat with a wretched headache, but if you need anything, call the house. Gretchen will come to see if you would like dinner sent over to you. Feel free to use pool and tennis court when available.

> *Cordially,*
> *Amantha Farley*

" 'When available?' " Kim raised her eyebrows.

"Kim, don't be picky. It's very kind of her. She doesn't even know us."

"And probably still won't when we leave. Oh, well. Hey, look, there's a little fridge." She opened the door. "Milk. And there's the Sunkist orange."

"She's being very nice," Stella said firmly. She did not say that she couldn't imagine her own mother, or Kim's, inviting guests and leaving them so entirely to their own devices. Still, there were the other house guests. And it *was* nice of her to let the two of them use the guest house. "Remember when we played hide-and-seek in here?"

"Do I ever. It didn't look all gussied up like this, though."

Now that they were there, they were not quite sure what to do with themselves. As long as the four guests were at the pool, they couldn't swim. The guest house seemed airless. Stella opened all the windows, and they unpacked and hung up the few clothes they had brought.

"Let's eat the hamburgers," Kim said, stuffing a cookie into her mouth. "I'm perishing from hunger."

They ate the hamburgers, the milkshakes, all the cookies, some bananas that were in the refrigerator, and most of the pitcher of milk.

Kim looked at the blue telephone on the bedside table. "We could call the house and say we haven't eaten for three days."

"Are you still hungry?"

"Starving."

From her canvas tote bag Stella brought out two large Cadbury chocolate bars, one with hazelnuts, one with raspberry. "Choose." She held them behind her back, and Kim got the raspberry one.

"It seems so quiet," Stella said, after they had finished the chocolate bars.

"No TV. Not even a radio. Tomorrow I'll go home and get mine."

"How long does it take to recover from appendicitis?"

Kim shrugged. "I suppose five or six days anyway."

Stella frowned. "She'll be all right, won't she?"

"Naturally. You know how healthy Hen is."

"Let's call her up."

But when they got the floor nurse, she told them that Hen had gone to sleep. "Yes, she's fine. She talked with her mother a while ago. Everything's fine."

By the time the house guests had left the pool, it was getting dark. There was a light outside the door of the guest house, and a floodlight at each end of the pool, but they provided limited illumination that was almost swallowed up by the darkness of the nearby woods. It was a cloudy evening, with no stars showing, and every so often thunder rumbled in the distance.

"It's spooky out here," Kim said. "Listen. You can hear all the bug noises."

Stella was looking at the table beside the bed where she had seen the girl crying.

"What is it?" Kim said.

"I'm not sure. When I looked in and saw that girl, there was something else. You know how you see things out of the corner of your eye and they don't exactly register. . . ." She squinted and looked again. "I know. There was a picture on that table. In a frame. I remember it kind of drifted through my mind that it might be a Parris, and then I realized it wouldn't be, and I forgot about it."

"So?" Kim was scooping up the crumbs in the cookie bowl.

"It's gone."

Cautiously Stella opened a drawer and looked in.
"Snoopy," Kim said.

Stella looked guilty. "It's okay, it's empty. It's not like it was in their house." She tried another drawer. "Nothing in it at all except a pencil." She opened the drawer in the other bedside table. "Hey," she said. "There it is." She looked at it a minute, and then lifted it out. It was a five by seven enlargement of a snapshot, in a silver frame, showing a young man, perhaps nineteen or twenty, in white shorts, white sneakers, and a white cotton sweater with two bands of color outlining the V-neck. He was holding a tennis racket and smiling.

"Wow," Kim said. "Cute."

"I wonder who he is." Stella studied it. "He's got eyes like the little kid. David."

"Lots of people have blue eyes."

"But not that intense. He looks almost fierce, even when he's smiling."

"Probably Mr. Farley when young."

"No, this looks contemporary." She put it back in the drawer. "Oh, well. So what." She flopped on the bed, her arms under her head. "Doesn't it seem odd though that there are four house guests, aged twenty or twenty-one or whatever, and nobody in the family over sixteen?"

"Maybe Jennifer is really Lolita."

"Oh, sure. Jennifer is the Ice Maiden, that's who Jennifer is."

Kim looked surprised. "You don't usually say mean things about people."

"Okay, so I'm mean, and I'm being what my mom calls judgmental, but I do not like Jennifer Farley, and Jennifer Farley very obviously does not like me. Or you, either. She makes me feel the way an ameba must feel when some human eye stares at it through a microscope."

Kim crossed her legs and rocked back and forth on her bed. " 'I do not like thee, Doctor Fell, the reason why I cannot tell.' "

Stella straightened up. "I heard something. Like a splash. Do you think somebody's swimming?"

"I don't know, but I wish I'd thought of it first. I love to swim in the dark." Kim got up, went to the window and peered out, trying to adjust her vision to the darkness. "There is somebody swimming." She waited till the swimmer came into the arc of light from the pool spotlights. "It's that other guy, not Bill." After a minute she said, "Somebody else is there, not swimming, somebody scrunched down and talking to him."

Stella joined her at the window, and they watched the swimmer hoist himself out of the water. The second person was a man, but his back was to the girls, and they couldn't tell who it was.

The second person took something from his pocket and held it out. Instead of taking it, the guest, the one called Hank, took the man by the arm and drew him away from the light. Their silhouettes were only faintly visible. In a few minutes the man had gone, heading toward the wall and the road, and Hank had put on his terrycloth robe and was sitting beside the pool smoking a cigarette.

"I wonder who that was?" Kim said.

"It was George Foss," Stella said. "I'd know that shuffly walk anywhere."

They looked at each other. "George Foss," Kim said thoughtfully. She pushed the casement window open as far as it would go and leaned out, taking deep breaths. "The wind is from the wrong direction, but if it were easterly, I'll bet you anything you'd get a whiff of pot. I think Georgie Foss just made himself a sale."

Stella shrugged. "I hope that guy knows what he's doing. If Georgie sold it to him, it's likely to be two-thirds horse manure."

Kim giggled. Then she said, "Somebody's coming out."

They watched one of the girls come into the circle of light and go beyond it to where Hank sat. She sat down beside him and in a few minutes the glowing ends of two cigarettes were visible. The two smokers sat there for a long time, talking in low voices. Even

with the carrying power of the water, Kim and Stella could not hear anything that they said.

Keeping watch grew boring, and Kim turned away, looking for something more to eat in the fridge and not finding anything. Stella was about to leave the window too, but something stopped her.

"Kim, look." She pointed to a small shadow moving along the outer edge of the pool enclosure. The shadow kept in the dark and moved stealthily.

"It has to be David," Stella said. "Nobody else is so small."

"What's he doing?"

"Spying, it looks like."

"He ought to be in bed."

"I get the feeling that David seldom is where he ought to be."

They watched the shadow hunker down until it was nearly invisible to them. He was wearing a dark sweater or T-shirt, but his khaki shorts were visible. He crouched there a long time.

Suddenly a nearby flash of lightning streaked across the sky, followed almost at once by a roar of thunder and rain falling in huge drops. The two young people got up and ran for the house, and moments later David too headed for the house, but the watchers noticed that he didn't go in by the patio door. In seconds he was swallowed up in darkness and rain.

6

IN THE MORNING KIM FOUND A RAIN-SOAKED ROACH
that someone had dropped the night before. She carefully put it in an envelope and left it in the drawer
that held the young man's picture.

"What's that for?" Stella asked. "You're not taking
up pot, are you?"

"Evidence," Kim said.

"Of what?"

"How do I know? Somebody was smoking pot out
there last night. Two'll get you one they bought it
from Georgie Foss. It's useful sometimes to know
things like that."

"It's probably more barn sweepings than Acapulco
gold."

Kim practiced against the backboard on the tennis
court for an hour and then they went back to Stella's
house to check on the tropical fish and change their

clothes. Late in the morning Stella called the hospital to see how Hen was. When she hung up, she said, "Doing as well as can be expected. We can see her tomorrow if all goes well."

"Hospitals are just gold mines of information, aren't they?" Kim said. "Let's amble downtown and see what's going on."

In front of the post office Nicole swept down upon them, bristling with indignation. "You types," she said accusingly. "Why didn't you tell me Hen was here? And what's she here for anyway? Nobody will tell me anything."

"Somebody must have told you something," Kim said. "How'd you know she was here?"

"It was in the paper, Smarty. Under hospital news. I called up to see if it was our Harriet Norton, and the home address checked out. What's going on anyway?"

"Nothing is going on, Nicole," Stella said. "Hen came to stay with us while our parents are in Bermuda, and she came down with appendicitis."

"You could have told me."

A bit lamely Stella said, "Well, we would have, but it all happened so fast."

"So are you guys staying by yourselves? My mother would never let me—"

Stella interrupted. "Of course not. We're staying

in the guest house at the Parrises'. I mean the Farleys'."

"Oh." Stella studied them suspiciously. "How come?"

"Dr. Endicott arranged it." Stella was getting tired of Nicole's questions. "We have to go now."

Nicole smiled her smuggest smile. "I know something you don't know. About the Farleys."

"Good for you," Stella said shortly. "Come on, Kim."

Nicole raised her voice so they would be sure to hear her as they walked away. "They had a son in college. He OD'd at a fraternity party. He was named Joshua."

Both girls stopped short and turned back.

Nicole grinned. "I thought that would interest you." She folded her arms and waited for the questions.

"How do you know?"

"My mother found out."

"I'll bet she did," Kim said under her breath.

"It happened just a year ago. Those guys staying with them now were friends of his. Bill Webb, Anne somebody, Hank, and Alicia. Mr. Farley took his son's death terribly hard. He retired and sold his business, and he and Mrs. Farley spent nearly a year in Europe, trying to get over their grief. One of the girls that's there now was engaged to Joshua. Anne, I think. The two guys went to school with him at Exeter. Then to the same college, I forget which one, out in the Middle West."

Kim and Stella looked at each other. "Anne," Stella said. "That was why she was crying."

"That must be a picture of Joshua."

"Listen, if I'm giving you all this news, you could at least explain what you're talking about."

"I saw one of the girls crying," Stella said. It made her uncomfortable to stand here gossiping with Nicole, but she was glad of the information. In further conversation, however, it was clear that aside from the news that Mrs. Farley had suffered some sort of nervous breakdown after Joshua's death, Nicole had nothing else to offer. They left her as soon as they could manage it.

There was a message waiting for them from Mrs. Farley when they got back to the cabana in the late afternoon.

Dear Girls:
I hope you are enjoying your stay. If you need anything, just ask.

Cordially yours,
Amantha Farley

P.S. If you would care to join us for an informal barbecue supper around the pool at seven, we would love to have you. AF.

They looked at each other.

"Shall we go?" Stella asked Kim.

"Why not? It's bound to be more interesting than sitting here."

At first they were not sure that Kim's remark was true. Except for Bill Webb, who talked to them for a few minutes about the fishing in the river, and except for Mrs. Farley greeting them in a vague way almost as if she had forgotten who they were, no one paid any attention to them.

Mr. Farley had obviously sampled his gin and tonic several times before he came out to build up the charcoal fire, and Stella suspected that Mrs. Farley had either had several drinks or had taken a strong tranquilizer. "She seems really out of it," Stella said to Kim in a low voice.

Hank and Alicia sat side by side in deck chairs, holding hands and sipping their drinks. They seemed to be aware of no one except each other. Jennifer helped her father with the fire, and seemed to keep a watchful eye on her mother, but she said nothing to anyone. David was studying a drop of water on a glass slide, using his small monocular. He seemed totally absorbed. Anne sat in another deck chair, a little removed from the others, her head back and her eyes closed. She looked pretty in a white tennis dress. Bill sat cross-legged on the deck, watching Mr. Farley and talking about fish. Mr. Farley was barbecuing swordfish steaks on his big Webcor, and Bill was especially interested in the Finnish Rapala knife, designed for fileting fish. Mr. Farley was explaining about it in an unnecessarily loud, slightly thickened voice. It was the first time Stella and Kim had had a good look at him, and they were not impressed.

He was a man who had once been athletic and now had run to fat, soft and somehow unhealthy-looking. His thin blond hair was carefully combed to cover the bald spot on the top of his head, but the breeze kept disarranging it. He had pale gray eyes that at the moment were red-rimmed, as if he had not slept, or as if he had a severe hangover.

"Look-a-here," he boomed to Bill. "See where it's written on the blade? 'J. Something . . .' " He squinted at it. "Marthusu, it looks like. Finns have got weird names. See, here's where it was made, Rovaniemi, Finland. Handground, it says, see here? Handground stainless steel." He ran his forefinger along the sharp, curved blade. "Oops. Look at that, if you don't think it's wicked sharp." He held up his finger, where small droplets of blood oozed. Laughing, he called to his wife. "Look here, honey. I'm showing Bill how sharp the Finnish knife is, and whadda ya know, I cut myself."

Mrs. Farley shuddered and turned away. "Jennifer, get him a Band-aid."

"Before he bleeds all over the swordfish," Jennifer muttered. Not hurrying, she went inside.

Stella watched closely. If Mr. Farley did bleed on the fish, she did not intend to eat any. But he wrapped a handkerchief around his finger, and when Jennifer returned, he put on the Band-aid, letting the loose pieces of paper fall to the deck.

"Jen-Jen," he said in his loud voice, "bring out the multi-band radio. Cripes, we need some music around here. The place is dead."

Without comment Jennifer went into the house again, and when she came back, she had turned the radio on to an FM station that played rock.

"That's better," Mr. Farley said. He did an awkward little dance. Jennifer sat down with her back to him, facing toward the road.

"How embarrassing can he get," Kim murmured in Stella's ear. "If I didn't think Jennifer was such a snobby brat, I'd feel sorry for her."

The maid came out with a big bowl of potato salad and set it on a card table. She followed that with plastic plates and cups and saucers, paper napkins that had the Eiffel Tower on them, a wicker basket filled with rolls wrapped in a linen napkin. And finally she plugged a huge silver coffee percolator into a long extension cord that led to an outlet near the door of the house, and set the pot on the card table, too.

There were other enticing things on the table: pickled watermelon rind, stuffed olives, celery, cucumbers, and a red clay pot full of zucchini with tomatoes and cheese. The clay pot sat on a warmer connected to the long extension cord. As she went past Mr. Farley, she spoke to him.

"What's that?" he roared. "Oh, all right. Folks, our little lady here says you all be careful not to trip over that mess of cords. We don't want anybody falling into the pool in his Sunday best. Even if the jet set does do it." He laughed heartily, and Bill was the only one who managed a smile.

A little later, having hovered over the Webcor, he shouted, "Soup's on, folks. Come 'n get it."

David bobbed up first in line with his plate, until Jennifer spoke to him sharply and he pulled back to let the guests in ahead of him.

Stella and Kim held off until everyone else had been served, feeling themselves to be in a rather ambiguous position, not family, not quite guests. Mr. Farley peered at them as if he had no idea who they were, but he smiled his "Host" smile and made a joke about the swordfish. The girls retired to the far end of the pool.

Hank and Alicia were sitting on the diving board, still engrossed in each other. Anne was talking to David, probably about Stonehenge, Stella thought.

Jennifer sat silently beside her mother, glancing at her often as if anxious about her. Mrs. Farley had her plate, which Jennifer had brought her, but she was not eating. Jennifer said something to her, and with a start Mrs. Farley picked up her fork and took a bite of potato salad, then put the fork down again.

Kim whispered to Stella. "She looks spacey."

Stella shook her head, frowning. She was afraid someone would hear Kim. Maybe Mrs. Farley was on anti-depressants or something. She did look strange, as if she were not part of the scene at all. Stella thought of her own well-balanced, enthusiastic mother and was thankful. "I hope they're having a terrific time in Bermuda," she said.

Mr. Farley rapped his Finnish knife against his glass to get their attention. "Folks," he said, "I'd like to propose a toast." His voice had changed, and he suddenly seemed less drunk.

Jennifer said, "Dad—" and broke off.

He glanced at her. "I would like to propose a toast to a brilliant young man who left us just a year ago tonight." He lifted his glass. "To my son, Joshua Farley."

No one moved for a moment. Then Jennifer jumped up and ran into the house, tears streaming down her face. Mrs. Farley was sitting up straight, her attention caught at last.

"What?" she said. "What?"

Bill Webb lifted his glass and said solemnly, "To Josh."

Hank and Alicia exchanged glances, then raised their glasses. Anne was staring at Bill. "How dare you drink to Josh?" she said.

"Annie," he said reproachfully.

"How dare any of us?"

Carefully Mr. Farley said, "What do you mean, Anne?"

"She's overwrought," Hank said.

Alicia gave her hard, high giggle. "What a funny word. Does it mean to be wrought over?"

Anne spoke to Mr. Farley, who waited for her answer. "Doesn't it seem odd to you that Josh died of an overdose? *Josh?* He never even smoked pot. Josh dead of an overdose?"

Bill put his arm around her. "Easy, Annie. No histrionics. It just makes it harder for everybody."

"What do you mean?" Mr. Farley said to Anne. "What are you getting at?" Suddenly he seemed not at all drunk.

He's doing this on purpose, Stella thought; he got them together hoping this would happen.

Hank spoke up. "Annie, love, you're upset. It's a bad day for all of us."

"I am saying," she said in a clear voice, addressing Mr. Farley, "not that anyone meant to harm him, but they wanted to make a fool of him at that fraternity party. A lot of people were jealous of Josh. But he did die, and there is such a thing as manslaughter, isn't there?" Her voice broke.

"You're hysterical, Annie." Hank eased himself off the diving board and came over to her. "Bill and I were there. Nobody made Josh do anything he didn't want to do." He turned to Mr. Farley. "Really, sir, can you imagine Josh ever letting people make him do what he didn't want to do?"

"Not offhand," Mr. Farley said. He was frowning.

Mrs. Farley stood up abruptly, swayed a moment, and fainted. The glass she had been holding broke on the deck with a tinkle like wind chimes.

"Amantha!" Mr. Farley lifted the crumpled figure and took her into the house.

There was silence for a moment. Then Alicia said, in a light voice, "As we were saying. . . ."

Bill glanced at David and shook his head at Alicia. "Cool it, Allie. Let's drive into town and see if there's anything going on."

"There isn't." David's voice was clear. He sat on the grass beyond the deck, his arms wrapped around his knees. "There never is."

"I'm not going anywhere," Anne said. "Except inside." She went into the house.

Bill shrugged. Then he said, "Listen, there's a pool table in the rec room. Let's give it a try. And I'll tell you something. I think it's time we leveled with the Farleys."

Both Hank and Alicia looked as if they had been struck. "Don't be an *ass*, Bill," Hank said in a low voice.

Alicia and Hank followed Bill into the house. David didn't move, and for a minute or two Stella and Kim stayed where they were. Suddenly David jumped up and ran over to them.

"Have you read *Hamlet*," he said, "by William Shakespeare?"

"I have," Stella said.

Kim shook her head. "Why, David?"

"There is something rotten in the state of Denmark." He wheeled around and dove into the pool and swam a hard dog paddle to the other end, climbed out with water dripping from his shorts, and disappeared.

Kim stood up. "This is a very odd family," she said. "And I'm going to have some more potato salad."

They refilled their plates and took them back to the guest house.

"What do you make of all that?" Stella said.

"I think somebody or some people were trying to be funny at that party, and their idea of a blast was to feed acid to a guy like Joshua, who never took dope. They overdid it, and he died."

"And Mr. Farley brought these people here to see if he could find out who did it."

"Did he find out?"

Stella shrugged. "If he did, he's way ahead of me."

7

ABOUT AN HOUR LATER STELLA AND KIM WERE IN THEIR pajamas, Stella reading a Robert Parker mystery, and Kim doing the *Globe* crossword. Except for the maid, who had come out to the pool to clear away some of the dishes, no one had appeared again. Faintly from the house came the sounds of a stereo playing pop music.

"Anne seemed to be accusing somebody," Stella said.

"I've heard of people being given acid in orange juice and not knowing they got it." Kim shrugged. "Probably we'll never know. Anyway it won't bring Joshua back. The Farleys might as well face it."

"Revenge," Stella said. "Mr. Farley wants to get even with whoever caused his son's death. I don't think I blame him."

"What's a six-letter word for 'ruler?' "

"Monarch."

"That's seven letters."

Stella sat up straight. "Listen."

"What?"

"There's somebody out by the pool."

"Are the lights on yet?" Kim got out of bed and came over to the window.

"Yes. Can you see anything?"

Kim put her hands on either side of her eyes, trying to see. "Somebody's standing by the pool." She turned away a moment later, puzzled. "It's Patrick Moon."

"Patrick? Don't tell me he cleans the pool after dark!" She joined Kim at the window.

"Maybe he's planning to burgle the house. He's done time for burglary, you know."

"Let's go find out."

"In our pajamas?"

"We've got robes. Maybe we'll prevent a robbery and the Farleys will be so grateful, we'll get to use the pool whenever we want."

"*And* the tennis court," Kim said wistfully. She put on her robe and her white duck hat.

Stella laughed. "Don't you go anywhere without that crazy hat?"

"Not if I can help it."

Stella was looking out the window. "Hold it. Somebody's coming out of the house."

They watched as Bill and Mr. Farley came and stood near the diving board, in the beam of the pool light. Patrick Moon had disappeared as suddenly as he had come.

"He and Georgie do everything in cahoots," Kim said. "I bet he was buying or selling dope."

"Buying?" Stella looked at her thoughtfully.

They could hear the murmur of the two men's voices, carried across the water, but not the words. A moment later Hank and Alicia joined them, and Mr. Farley and Bill moved apart.

Alicia's voice was high and shrill. "Hey, are you guys going swimming? I think that's a great idea." She tripped over the electrical cords that had not been cleared away, and Mr. Farley caught her arm.

His voice had changed to the loud joking tone he had used at the barbecue. "Watch it, little lady," he said. "You don't want to go swimming that bad, do you?"

Alicia laughed and hung onto his arm. She was wearing dark blue sailcloth pants and a black T-shirt, and when she stepped out of the circle of light, she was hard to see. "Aren't I the clumsy one," she said. "You saved my life, Mr. Farley."

"She sounds high," Kim whispered.

Mrs. Farley came out of the house, and a moment later Anne followed. "Ah, here you all are," Mrs.

Farley said. "How wise. It's gorgeous out here to-night. Would anyone like beer?"

"Mrs. F. looks okay now," Stella said.

"Conscious anyway."

Alicia teetered on the rim of the pool, and Hank grabbed her. "No, Allie," he said laughing, "you cannot walk on water."

She thrust her arms high and threw her head back. "I can do anything. I am Alicia the All-Powerful."

Mrs. Farley walked toward the house. "I'll see about the beer." She slid open the patio door.

Suddenly the lights went out, plunging the pool area into dense blackness. Voices squealed in surprise. Mr. Farley shouted something. Someone struck a match that immediately went out. In its moment of flair Kim and Stella saw the people huddled together at the edge of the pool like blind men touching each other for orientation. Then in the darkness there was a confused movement toward the house.

"That stupid Moon," Mr. Farley was saying. "I told him to fix that connection."

In a few moments they seemed to have gone inside. The pool was quiet. Stella yawned and went back to bed. Kim was following when she stopped suddenly.

"What is it?" Stella said.

Kim listened intently, then shook her head. "I don't know. I thought I heard a splash. I don't see anything though. I guess I'm hearing things."

Stella giggled. "Maybe Patrick Moon is taking a late evening swim. Hey, maybe he committed suicide."

"No such luck."

In less than an hour the pool lights went on again, and a minute later someone screamed.

Sleepily Kim and Stella pulled on their robes and approached the pool area with caution, hoping to see what was going on without being noticed. They soon realized that there was no need for caution: no one was at all interested in them.

Anne stood by the diving board with her hands clasped in front of her. Hank had his arm protectively around Alicia, who was sobbing and saying, "Oh, no!" over and over again. Jennifer had her mother by the hand, the two of them standing motionless, staring at the pool, where Mr. Farley stood in chest-high water, holding Bill Webb's body in his arms.

David came running out of the house, stopped, gasped, and drew back against the windowboxes, almost out of sight in the darkness.

"Let me help you, sir," Hank said, though he made no move.

"No," Mr. Farley said sharply. "He's dead."

There was that thin scream again, and Stella saw that it came from Alicia. Anne had pressed both hands against her mouth, and her body sagged, as if she were suddenly an old woman.

Mr. Farley walked with difficulty through the water to the edge of the pool and carefully laid Bill's body on the deck.

Jennifer spoke suddenly, in a loud, reasonable voice. "How could it have happened? People don't just jump into a pool and drown."

"Perhaps he hit his head," her mother said.

"I thought he'd gone to bed," Hank said.

None of them made a move to go closer to the body. They stood in place, like a frieze. Kim and Stella, who were closer to Mr. Farley, saw him turn his back on the others and bend over the body. It struck Stella that in death or in the artificial light, Bill's body had lost its healthy, tanned look and had taken on a sickly yellow cast. Her stomach felt suddenly queasy.

Mr. Farley straightened up and turned toward the others. "Jennifer, call the chief of police." He glanced at Kim and Stella, although he had not seemed aware of their presence before. "What is the man's name?"

"Robert Blake," Stella said.

Jennifer turned toward the house, then paused. "What shall I tell him? That . . . that someone drowned?"

Her father took a moment to answer. "Tell him Bill Webb has been murdered."

There was a moment of total silence, and then Alicia screamed again, that thin, piercing sound. Stella wanted to shake her.

"Murdered?" Jennifer said, in an unbelieving voice.

"Come on, Mr. Farley," Hank said. "You can't mean that."

"No?" Mr. Farley's wet trousers and shirt clung to him, and Stella could see that he was shivering. "My fish knife is plunged to the hilt in his chest."

For the second time that evening Mrs. Farley fainted.

8

ROBERT BLAKE LOOKED AT THE GROUP ASSEMBLED IN
the Farleys' living room. He was a tall, good-looking
man, who often played golf with Stella's father. She
had given his name automatically when Mr. Farley
asked her, because Bobby Blake was the smartest man
by far on the town's six-man police force; he was in
fact, however, only assistant chief. The chief was
Haskell Ames, a man in his late sixties, who had been
the town's only constable years ago, and who had
regularly been re-elected chief when the force en-
larged. Haskell was a habit. Everyone liked him and
smiled tolerantly when they spoke of him, but they
all knew he was not the smartest man in Essex County.
He was good with kids, he could talk juveniles out of
vandalism they were bent on, and he was good with
the habitual drunks who so often occupied the town's

one-cell jail in the basement of the Town Hall. But Hercule Poirot, Haskell wasn't.

Watching Bobby Blake's calm, methodical manner, Stella hoped she hadn't caused any hurt feelings by not naming Haskell. Probably he was secretly glad not to have been routed out of his comfortable bed at odd hours of the night. And Bobby was going about his job as if he investigated murders every week. He had come at once last night, looked at the body, sent for the medical examiner, called Haskell to inform him. Now in the early morning, after what had probably been a restless night for all of them, with part-time cop Phil Maloney taking notes, he was questioning the group, including the maid, the cook, and Stella and Kim. The only person missing was David, whom Stella had not seen since Mr. Farley's announcement that Bill had been murdered. No one seemed to notice that he was not there. Probably too scared to come down, Stella thought, though she would have expected him to be more curious than frightened.

"Then almost all of you were out at the pool, with the lights on, at—" Bobby looked at the sparse notes he had made for himself. ". . . approximately ten fifteen." He looked politely from one to another.

"We weren't there," Kim said. "Stell and I had gone to bed, but we were awake."

"Thanks, Kim." He smiled at her. To Mr. Farley

he said, "How did everyone happen to come outside just then?"

Mr. Farley's face was pale and drawn. "Bill and I had gone first, to be alone. I wanted to question him about—" He hesitated and glanced at his wife. "—my son's death. He was there, you see, when Josh died."

"I see." Bobby looked at Hank. "You were there too, sir, I understand, when Joshua Farley died."

"Yes," Hank said. "All four of us were. Of course, it was quite a long time ago."

"One year," Mr. Farley said. "One year to the day."

"And the rest of you joined Mr. Farley and Mr. Webb outside after . . . how many minutes would you say?"

"Maybe five," Mr. Farley said. "Bill and I never got to finish our talk."

Bobby looked at Anne and Alicia, who sat close together on a leather loveseat. Anne was deathly pale, and Alicia looked different without makeup.

Anne said, in a low voice, "Somebody said somebody was going swimming. Then somebody else—I think it was Hank—said, 'Let's go out and get some fresh air.' So we did."

"And suddenly the lights went out." Bobby kept his voice calm, as if nothing was surprising in what he was being told.

"Yes," Mr. Farley said. "We've had a bit of trouble with those lights. Patrick Moon promised to see to them."

"He was here," Stella said.

Everyone looked at her, and she felt herself turn red. She hated to speak up in front of a lot of people.

"Who was here, dear?" Mr. Farley said.

"Patrick Moon."

"When, Stella?" Bobby said.

"Just before Mr. Farley and Bill came out. He disappeared when he heard them coming."

There was a moment of silence. Then Hank said, "You must have imagined it. I looked out there myself just before Bill and Mr. Farley went out. There was nobody there."

"We saw him," Kim said.

Mr. Farley looked unhappy. "Why would Patrick Moon be here at ten o'clock at night?"

"He wouldn't," Jennifer said. "Not Mr. Moon. Not to do any work. He's too lazy. Unless he came to sell somebody some pot."

Stella heard someone gasp, but she wasn't sure who it was.

"Were people here buying pot?" Bobby asked, in a pleasant, conversational tone.

"Of course not," Mr. Farley said shortly.

"Ha!" Jennifer said.

"Jennifer, you're upsetting your mother," Mr. Farley said sharply. He looked at Bobby and shook his head. "These youngsters. Imagination runs away with 'em."

"I have a roach that somebody dropped by the pool," Kim said. "It's not an imaginary roach."

Again there was that tiny moment of silence. Then Alicia spoke. "Can you prove it isn't your own, honey?"

Kim looked startled. "I don't smoke pot. Stella saw me pick it up. It was all wet from the rain."

Gently Bobby steered the conversation back to the subject of Bill's death. There were more questions, and Stella thought she was going to die of hunger. At last he stood up. "That's all for now, folks. Chief Haskell will want you to stick around for a while. Thank you for your cooperation. 'Preciate it."

When he reached the door, Jennifer said, "My little brother has disappeared."

"Jennifer, for heaven's sake!" her father said. "You know that kid. He's around somewhere."

"I can't find him."

"Officer," Mr. Farley said, "my son wanders around a lot. I'm sure he's all right."

Bobby looked at them thoughtfully for a moment. Then he nodded and went out.

"There will be breakfast in the dining room, in about fifteen minutes?" Mr. Farley looked at the maid, who nodded and scuttled out of the room. "I'm terribly sorry for all this bother, but, as they say, we may as well relax and enjoy it." Then it seemed to strike him that he had said something awkward. "Figure of speech, of course. We can't enjoy anything after what has happened."

As Kim and Stella left the room, they both looked back at Mrs. Farley. She sat staring into space, as if unaware of the others.

They caught up with Bobby Blake.

"Mr. Blake," Stella said, "can we go off the premises? We're awful hungry, and we're not exactly guests."

He smiled at her. "What are you exactly, Stell?"

"Sort of camping out here." She explained.

"Sure, you can leave. Just don't leave town." He winked at them. "Say, Kim, let me have that roach, will you?"

When she had given it to him, and they were riding their bikes toward Mrs. Garrison's coffee shop, Kim said, "Bobby believed me anyway."

It was still early, but Mrs. Garrison's was open from five o'clock till midnight. They ordered the biggest breakfasts on the menu and sat clutching their stomachs and trying to be patient while the eggs and ham and hash browns and toast were prepared for them.

It was not until they had eaten every bite that they looked at each other and Kim said, "Who did it?"

9

_____

STELLA SHOOK HER HEAD. IT SEEMED TO HER THAT JUST about everyone at the Farleys' had a motive. Mr. Farley had gone to the trouble of getting Joshua's friends up here. If he had discovered that Bill gave Joshua the acid that killed him, he could very well have taken his revenge. Mrs. Farley was odd enough to do almost anything, and Joshua, after all, was her beloved son, too. Intense Jennifer was an enigma.

"And the others," she said, continuing her train of thought aloud. "Anne was in love with Joshua. She must hate whoever caused his death. As for Hank and Alicia, if they had something to hide. . . ."

"In other words, everybody's suspect," Kim said.

"Except David. He couldn't have done it unless he had a ladder."

At that moment Barney Sellers, the town clerk, came in for his morning coffee. "Heard about the

(79)

murder out to the Parris place?" he said to Mrs. Garrison.

Her eyes widened. "Murder! Goodness sake, no."

Three other local businessmen came in, arguing about whose turn it was to buy.

"You guys heard about a murder?" Mrs. Garrison demanded before they even sat down.

They had not. All of them listened attentively while Barney gave a succinct description of the event.

"Maybe he got high and committed suicide," one of the men said. "I've heard of that. Don't know what they're doin' when they get all hyped up."

"It'd be kind of awkward to stick a fish fileting knife into your own heart," Barney said drily. "Got to be easier ways."

Mrs. Garrison's avid glance moved to Stella and Kim. "Aren't you two kids sleeping over, out to the Parrises, while your folks are gone?"

Mr. Whitcomb, who owned the hardware store, slapped the counter. "That's it," he said. "Kim and Stell did it. Fell in love with this feller from away, and when he spurned 'em, they done him in." The other men guffawed.

"That's not all that funny, Mr. Whitcomb," Kim said. "Not if you've seen the body with that knife sticking. . . ." She didn't finish.

Mr. Whitcomb looked abashed. "Guess you're right, Kim. I apologize. Just joking."

"Let's go," Kim said to Stella. They slid their money across the counter toward Mrs. Garrison and left, aware that they had suddenly become celebrities.

"People are ghoulish," Kim said, as they wheeled their bikes out toward Stella's house.

"They don't think," Stella said. "You know Mr. Whitcomb, anything for a laugh."

"Some laugh."

They remembered that it was trash collection day. Kim helped Stella wheel out the two metal trash cans that were in the garage, and then they went over to Kim's house and put out hers.

"I was thinking," Stella said. "It would be interesting to know just how friendly Joshua Farley was with Bill and Hank. Besides being in the same fraternity and having gone to the same prep school. If they were really such buddies and they knew who caused his death, wouldn't they report it? I'd report it as fast as I could if somebody did a thing like that to you."

"I would too, but fraternity brothers, that's some kind of weird relationship, like belonging to the Masons. One for all and all for one. Blood brothers."

"Just the same. . . ." Stella was quiet with her thoughts for a while. Then she said, "Jeff Eaton was in that class at Exeter."

"So? Jeff Eaton is gone abroad for the summer. He's not even in this country."

"I wonder if he had a yearbook. Prep schools must have yearbooks, the same as high schools."

"What would that prove?"

"I don't know, but let's find out." She led the way down the main road to a large driftwood-gray reproduction of a saltbox house and hurried to the front door before she lost her nerve.

Jeff Eaton's mother was nice. She and Stella's mother went to antique auctions together sometimes. She greeted the girls cordially and asked if they had heard from their parents.

"Not yet. Mrs. Eaton, this is a funny question, but I wonder if Jeff had a yearbook the year he graduated from Exeter."

"A yearbook? Yes, I believe he did. I guess it's still in his room. Why, dear?"

"Well, it's kind of like a treasure hunt, in a way. . . ." Stella gave Mrs. Eaton a wide, innocent smile.

"We just need to borrow it for a few hours," Kim said. "We'll take good care of it."

Mrs. Eaton smiled. "Just a minute. I'll see if I can find it."

She was back in about five minutes, blowing dust off the top of the pages. "I ought to get in there and give that room a good cleaning. Well, one of these days." She handed the annual to Stella. "I hope you find your treasure."

They thanked her and sped back to Stella's house.

Stella looked at her watch when they were inside. "First we call Hen, okay?"

"Do we tell her about the murder?"

"Not yet. She'll worry." She dialed the hospital number and asked for Hen's room. She was connected right away. Hen sounded rather faint, but she insisted she was fine.

"This afternoon I get to dangle my legs."

"Big deal. When do you get to go off the diving board?"

Hen laughed and said, "Ouch! Not yet. Are you kids all right?"

"Great. We're coming to see you this afternoon."

"They won't let you stay long. I'm not supposed to talk very long."

"We'll bring you something nice."

Kim talked to her for a minute, and then they hung up and settled down with the annual. "What are we looking for?"

"I don't know." Stella leafed through the pages. "Wow, what a lot of neat guys."

"Don't you wish you could go to Exeter? Hey, look, there's the prophecy pages. Look for Farley, Joshua."

"Here he is. He really was good-looking, wasn't he? Looks nice, too. What a way to go." She read the lines under the picture. " 'Our class president, Josh

Farley, is destined to go on filling high office. First in the Commonwealth, first in the U.S. Senate, maybe first in the White House? And always first in the hearts of his countrywomen. Make a good end run for it, Josh. We're behind you.'"

"That's sad," Kim said. "That's really sad."

Stella turned the pages to the W's. " 'Bill Webb, bound to head up some big corporation. And he'll make it work. No conventional company man, he, but a dynamo of ambition and originality. Nothing holds our Willie back.' "

"Well, so far they're batting zero," Kim said. "What does it say about Hank? Or didn't he go there, too?"

"Yes, here he is. 'Hank Paynter, Man of the Year, any year. Always in there slugging away. Hank won't take no for an answer. He'll wheel and deal his way to the top, our Hank will. If Farley is president, Hank will be VP, maybe with a plan up his sleeve for impeaching the pres? Don't turn your back, Farley.' "

Kim and Stella looked at each other.

"Wow," Kim said. "I guess there was no love lost."

"But being competitive doesn't mean he was ready to commit murder."

Kim pushed her hat onto the back of her head. She had already begun to tan. Stella, who burned, envied her.

Kim leafed through the yearbook. Under Athletics

there was a fuzzy snapshot of Hank s
ball. "He was never too good, was he? A
holds that racket, like he's going to chop w

Stella pointed out a group shot of five y
in basketball uniforms. One of them was Josh
around boy."

The Honors section showed Joshua with top honors; Bill and Hank were not mentioned.

Stella put on her dark glasses and stared out the window. "Do you think Bill was in love with Anne?"

Kim shrugged. "Who knows."

"Anne. Anne would know."

"So?"

"What if Anne, who was in love with Joshua, and Bill, who was in love maybe with Anne—" She broke off. "Oh, I don't know."

Kim said, "What if Anne and Bill really cared about Joshua and wanted Mr. Farley to know who was responsible for his death . . . and what if Hank and Alicia didn't want Mr. Farley to be told. . . ." She stopped, frowning. "No, that doesn't add up. If Joshua died of an overdose, even Mr. Farley finding out who did it isn't any great threat. I mean, whoever was responsible is going to swear it was an accident whether it was or not. So back to square one."

"That's right. I suppose different people have differt tolerances to drugs, same as alcohol. My mother starts to stagger if you hold a glass of wine under her nose." She got up and rinsed out the glasses that she and Kim had been drinking root beer from. "Let's return the yearbook and then mosey over to the Farleys in case there's any news."

Patrick Moon was working at the pool. He had drained the water out and was refilling it. As they walked up, he glowered at them.

"Hi, Mr. Moon." Kim put her finger to the brim of her hat in a gesture just short of impudent.

"Look here," he said. "How come you kids told them lies about me? I had a heck of a time convincing Bobby I wasn't nowhere around here. In the middle of the night, for pity's sake! What would I be doin' in the middle of the night?"

"We saw you, Mr. Moon," Stella said.

He took threatening steps toward her. "You didn't see me, and if you don't quit saying you did, I'm gonna . . . I'm . . ."

"You're going to what?"

"Oh, come on, Kim," Stella said, walking away.

But Kim stood her ground. "What will you do if we don't lie for you?"

He half lifted his right hand as if to hit her, his face dark with anger. "I'll git even, that's what I'll do." He stared at her with hard eyes.

"I don't think you'd better harm us," Kim said calmly. "Because then you'd be in real trouble." She turned on her heel and followed Stella.

She found her standing just inside the door, holding in her hand a sheet of cheap typing paper on which someone had pasted letters cut from a newspaper. She held it out. The letters, pasted on crookedly, some lower case, some capitals, read:

KEeP yoUR NOSeS OUT OF OTheR PEOpLe's busiNESs OR ELSe.

10

HASKELL AMES STOOD BEHIND BOBBY BLAKE IN THE
big room in the Town Hall that was the police headquarters. "Not too neat of a job," he said, running
his hand over the bald spot on top of his head. He
was looking at the message.

"Looks like somebody was in a hurry," Bobby
said. "How long were you girls away from the Farley
place this morning?"

"We left right after you did, to get breakfast. We
just went back now, and found this." Stella told him
too what Patrick Moon had said to them.

"Well, old Pat Moon," Haskell said. "He ain't got
good sense. Probably he *was* there—"

Kim interrupted. "Mr. Ames, we *know* he was
there. We saw him."

"All right, he was there. And the only thing in the

world I can think of that'd bring him there at that hour is like you said, peddling dope or buying it. Kinda foolhardy, but then, Patrick don't know his— uh—derrière from his elbow, as the French say."

"We'd better send Phil over to Pat's place to take a look around," Bobby Blake said. "Now, while he's at the Farleys'."

"Can't do 'er without a search warrant," Haskell Ames said.

"Oh, Pat's Mabel will let Phil in. She's not all that devoted to Patrick. She filed a complaint last fall, remember? Said he beat the bejabbers out of her."

"You girls are doing fine," Haskell said. "You hear anything more, let us know, all right?"

"What about the message?" Stella said.

"Oh, Pat's work, I'd say. Trying to scare you off. We'll keep it here, if you don't mind." Bobby put it in his desk drawer.

The girls headed for the door.

Bobby's voice stopped them. "When are your folks coming home?"

Stella told him.

"And that girl that's supposed to look after you, when's she getting out of the hospital?"

"In a few days. Why?

"Well, I don't 'spose your folks would be thrilled to death at your choice of a safe place to stay. Why don't you move on back to your own house, and I'll have one of the boys keep an eye on you."

"Is it okay if we move back tomorrow?" Kim said. "I want to work on the Farleys' backboard this afternoon."

"Well, all right. But if anything worries you, give a holler. Phil will be standing on watch by the main entrance."

As they went out, they heard Haskell say, "Guess we'd better have a heart-to-heart talk with Georgie Foss, too, while we're about it. He and Pat are thicker'n thieves."

Stella and Kim had lunch at the A&W and then went to see Hen. They had bought her a large can of Almond Roca and a new mystery story.

"I hope she can chew this Roca," Stella said.

Kim, who had chosen it, said, "It's her appendix she had out, not her teeth."

They found Hen looking pale but sitting up in bed. "As long as I don't take too deep a breath and don't laugh and don't jump around," she said, "I'm fine." There were several large bouquets of flowers on her bureau. "My mom sent those spring flowers. Aren't they pretty? And you'll never guess who sent the violets." She grinned at them. "Nicole."

"She would," Kim said.

"Well, it was very sweet and thoughtful." Hen nodded toward a newspaper clipping beside her. "She also sent me the news about the death at the Farley place. What's it all about?"

Relieved to talk about it, they told her all they knew. She listened, frowning in concentration.

"I don't like having you there. Darn it, I wish I could get out of here." Hen winced at a pain.

"It's just till tomorrow. We're perfectly all right," Stella said. "There'll be a cop there all night."

And Kim said, "Actually we wouldn't have missed it for anything."

They didn't stay long, because Hen was obviously tiring. They left with promises to be careful.

"Whatever that means," Kim said afterward. "Careful of what?"

They went back to the Farley place right from the hospital. The pool sparkled with clean water, and Patrick Moon was nowhere in sight. Hank and Alicia were playing tennis, and Anne was stretched out on the pool deck, in dark glasses and a big floppy hat. She seemed to be asleep. Mr. Farley came out of the house, got into his car, and drove away.

"Let's go call on Mrs. Farley," Stella said, changing course. "Before you get started working out on the tennis court."

"What for?"

"Just to see if she's all right, if there's anything we can do for her. She must be in kind of a state of shock, after all." As they neared the house, Stella said, "I wish we could get a look at Hank's and Alicia's rooms."

"Why?"

"People on dope probably have some paraphernalia lying around. You know, that stuff they sell in head shops."

"I'll bet Bobby Blake has already thought of that."

Mrs. Farley herself answered their ring at the doorbell. She had not recently applied her makeup, and she looked strangely washed-out, faded. She stared at them blankly for a moment, then said, "Oh, it's the girls from the village. Come in." Her hands went to her hair. "I look a fright. But come in anyway. Would you like some orange pop?"

"No, thank you, Mrs. Farley," Stella said. "We don't want to bother you. We just wanted to see if there's anything we could do for you."

"Do for me?" She seemed bewildered by the question. Then she said, "There is one thing. My son David has not been back here since . . . well, since last night, when there was all that confusion. You might tell him if you see him that I want him to come home now. It's important." Her pale eyebrows went up in an anxious frown.

"Of course we will. He's probably down along the river someplace. He likes to climb the trees."

"Yes. I want to see him."

There was an awkward pause.

"Well," Kim said, "we just wanted to see if you were all right."

"You don't know how much I appreciate that. I really do." Mrs. Farley clasped her hands tightly together. She was wearing a huge emerald on her right hand and an elaborate diamond on her ring finger, with her diamond-studded wedding ring.

The girls turned to go away, and then Stella said, "Oh, maybe we could take Hank that other racket he wanted. As long as we're here."

Kim looked blank for only a moment. Then she said, "Hey, that's right. Which way is his room, Mrs. Farley?"

"Hank's and—" She stopped. "Hank and Bill shared the room at the end of the wing." She pointed vaguely. "You *will* tell David if you see him?"

"Yes, we really will."

Stella and Kim sped down the long hall to the bedroom at the end. No one was in sight. They hesitated a moment, but the door was open.

"Come on," Stella said, and stepped inside. There were twin beds, both of them made up. Bill's clothes hung in a closet on one side of the room, Hank's in the other. A copy of *Playboy* lay on one of the beds, and there was an empty beer bottle on the floor.

Swiftly the girls looked at everything they could find, without actually touching things. They peered up at closet shelves, cautiously opened bureau drawers. There was nothing they could see that suggested even marijuana, let alone more powerful drugs. Stella looked at the empty wastepaper basket.

"It's just occurred to me," she said, and stopped short.

A shadow fell across the room. The girls spun around.

Hank was leaning against the doorframe, his hands in his shorts pockets, and an odd smile on his face. His eyes were not smiling, however. "Well," he said. "This is such a big house, I'll bet you kids got lost. Thought you were going into your own little guest house, didn't you, and here you are in my room." He took his hands out of his pockets, still smiling that dangerous smile. "If it isn't rude to ask a direct question, *what are you doing here?*" He came into the room, and both girls instinctively took a few steps backward.

Stella felt the footboard of one of the beds pressing into her back. She decided that truthfulness was the only option they had. "We were looking at Bill Webb's things."

"Why?"

"Well, we know we saw Patrick Moon here just a short time before Bill was killed, and we wondered if he was trying to sell Bill some dope."

"And if he was or if he was not is that some concern of yours?" He was standing close to them now, and his hands were clenched.

"I guess not really," Stella said.

"We were just trying to help Bobby Blake find clues," Kim said.

He glanced around the room. "And did you find any?"

Stella shook her head.

He spoke in a low voice, with his teeth clenched. "Then get the hell out of here, and if I ever catch you snooping around the Farleys' house again, I'll advise them to have you arrested."

They stepped carefully around him. When they got to the door, he added one more remark. "You're a pair of ghouls. My friend is not yet in his grave, and you come here like vultures."

Stella threw him one last look and hurried away, Kim at her heels. When they were out of the house, she said, "The awful thing is, he's right. I shouldn't have thought of doing that. I hadn't looked at it from his point of view, or the Farleys'. Bill was Hank's friend. He must be feeling terrible."

Kim shrugged. "So we goofed."

"I deceived Mrs. Farley and took advantage of her."

"Look, we made a mistake. All right. It's over. What are we going to do next? I better not be seen on that tennis court for a while."

"Maybe we could go down to the river and look for David. That would relieve Mrs. Farley's mind, if we found him."

"I don't see David getting found unless he wants to be," Kim said, "but we can give it a try."

11

THEY SEARCHED ALONG THE RIVER FOR A LONG TIME,
calling David, but there was no response. An empty
orange pop bottle and a small paper bag from the
A&W, crumpled and half-hidden by a heap of pine
needles, were the only signs of recent human activity.
But, as Kim pointed out, the Farleys were not the
only people in the world whose taste seemed to run
to orange pop, and in the warm weather anybody
could have been picnicking alongside the river. In
fact, as she said it, a canoe came into view, a young
man, whom they knew slightly, was paddling from
the stern in long, slow sweeps, and a pretty girl,
whom they didn't know, sat on a canvas cushion,
trailing her fingers in the water.

The man said, "Hi," to the girls, and after a moment, Stella said to him, "Uh, you didn't happen to

see a little boy upstream, did you? About nine years old?"

He shook his head. "Nope."

The young woman smiled. "Afoot or a-horseback?"

"What? Oh, on foot."

"The only people we've seen were some other canoeists," the young man said. "Sorry."

"Well, thanks anyway."

Stella was peering up into any trees they came upon that were big enough to support a boy. Many of the trees were half-grown willows, not sturdy enough for climbing.

"He's probably hidden somewhere, watching us hunt," Kim said.

"You can hardly blame him. What kid wants to hang around home when they've just fished a body out of the pool?"

"Well, actually, I'd have thought David would. He struck me as being more inquisitive than squeamish."

Stella sank down onto the warm pine needles. "Well, he doesn't seem to be here. Gosh, I'm sleepy."

"Me too. Our biological time clocks are all screwed up. We've been up for—"

"—for months, it feels like." Stella closed her eyes, and in three minutes she was sound asleep.

Kim started to doze too, but a sudden thought struck her, and she sat bolt upright. There was something she had to do. She hated to wake Stella, so she scribbled a note on a piece of torn paper that she found in her pocket:

Stell, I'll be back in a few minutes.
Wait for me.

Kim

Then she walked back to the place where they had left their bikes, got hers, and rode fast down the loop road. Just before she came to the Farleys', she veered off on a narrow dirt road that bordered the property. That road in turn bisected an alley that ran along the back.

From here the house was not visible, although it was not in fact far away. As she had expected, there were three trash cans lined up beside the alley. It was garbage collection day, and thank goodness they did this end of town last. Hank's Audi was parked in the cemented half-circle bordering the alley.

Quickly and methodically she searched the first two cans, turning up her nose at the stink of rotting garbage. At least the Farleys' cook was neat enough to use big plastic bags, so she didn't have to touch the stuff.

There was a lot of trash paper, old newspapers, old magazines. (The Farleys subscribed, she noticed, to *Time*, the Sunday *New York Times*, the *Boston*

Globe, Harpers, and *Business Week.* She wondered if anyone read them all.)

It was fairly uninteresting trash. An old toothbrush, a toothpaste tube rolled up from the bottom and squeezed dry, quite a few vodka bottles and two Dry Sack sherry bottles, lots of pop bottles, a snapshot torn in half that showed the Farleys when David was still a baby. She put that in her pocket. You never knew when something might become significant. Like who tore it up and why?

She dumped all the stuff back and went to the third barrel. This looked like one that the bedroom wastebaskets had been emptied into. A broken comb. A small, thin alarm clock that had a broken mainspring. She put the clock in her pocket. You could always get a new mainspring.

She was nearly at the bottom when she found what she was looking for, and something else interesting that she had not thought of looking for. First, there was a disposable syringe. She sniffed at it, but there was no smell. She pocketed it. And she picked out the pieces of her second find, a copy of the News of the Week section of the *Times,* which had been cut into in many places. There were gaps where words had been removed. Triumphantly she folded the paper and put it inside her T-shirt. At least she could be pretty sure now that someone in the Farley household had put together the message left in the guest house. Not that that narrowed the field much, but at least it eliminated Patrick Moon and Georgie Foss.

Just as she was about to get on her bike, she thought she heard a sound, like someone stepping on a dry twig. But peering through the border of trees into the sloping green lawn, she couldn't see anyone. Probably imagined it. She got on her bike and rode back to the woods to tell Stella.

But when she got there, Stella was gone.

12

"I DIDN'T MEAN TO SCARE YOU," STELLA SAID, WHEN Kim finally found her some distance upriver. "I was coming back. But I heard somebody singing, a boy's voice, and I was sure it was David."

"But you didn't find him."

"No, but look." She guided Kim to a small area between two big trees, where half a dozen upended stones stood in a circle. "Dolmens."

"Come again?"

"Dolmens, like Stonehenge. Megaliths. Rocks standing on end in a pattern. Sometimes to mark a tomb. Remember that article in the *Geographic?*"

Kim studied the arrangement of stones and the smoothed-over earth that they surrounded. "Well, it's not big enough to bury anybody."

"No, but look." Stella picked up a dark blue feather. "Blue jay. I think he buried a dead jay."

"Oh, that nutty kid. Where the heck is he then?"

"Probably somewhere watching us. When is the summer solstice?"

"How do I know?"

"I think it's June twenty-second or around there. When the noon sun seems to stand still. Fred Hoyle thinks Stonehenge was meant to predict eclipses."

"How come you know all this?"

"I did a term paper on it." Stella picked up a flat rock that lay beside one of the stones. "This might have been meant for a lintel, but it isn't quite long enough."

"So move the rocks closer together." Kim put out her hand to one of the stones.

"No, don't. You'll destroy the proportions, and I think David really worked this out. That's the altar stone in the middle."

"David the Druid."

Stella shook her head. "Stonehenge was built, they think, a thousand years before the Druids."

Kim stared down at the circle. "It's spooky."

Stella was peering up into the leafy branches of the big willow. She raised her voice and spoke distinctly. "David, if you're listening, please go home at least long enough so your mom will know you're all right. She's worried. She's got enough to worry about without you." She stood in a listening attitude. Then she shook her head. "I felt he was here before, but I don't feel it now."

"You're getting spooky yourself," Kim said. "How can you feel people you can't see?"

"I don't know, but I think you can." She turned her attention to Kim. "Where did you go anyway?"

Kim showed her the cut-up newspaper and the syringe.

"We'd better give these to Bobby."

Kim agreed, and they biked into town to the police office. Bobby Blake was not there, but they left their evidence, with a note to explain where they had been found.

"Tomorrow is June twenty-second," Stella said. "Let's go by the library. There's a book I want to look at."

She checked out Fred Hoyle's *On Stonehenge* and went back to her house for a while. Kim decided it was safe to go to the Farleys' tennis court so she went off there.

"I'll join you there in an hour," Stella said. "I want to make some fudge for Hen."

When she arrived at the guest house, bringing part of the fudge for themselves, Kim had just come in. Stella tossed the Stonehenge book on the table.

"Golly, what a lot of *work!*"

"What was?"

"Stonehenge. Those stones were about twenty feet

long, seven or eight feet wide, and they moved them two hundred miles."

Kim bit into a piece of fudge. "That's impossible."

"No, they did. On wooden sledges. The BBC re-enacted it a few years ago. The old people, the pre-Druids or whoever they were, dug up the ground with deer antlers. Archeologists have found the broken pieces of antler." She looked out the window with a faraway gaze. "I think it would be kind of cool to be an archaeologist. Maybe I'll give it a whirl some day."

Kim looked over her shoulder at one of the book's illustrations. "It must have taken them a while."

"About a thousand years."

"Wow! No planned obsolescence there."

They made themselves a tuna fish salad for their supper, called Hen to make sure she still felt all right, and then went to sit by the pool in the long summer twilight. But they found Bobby Blake in a canvas chair talking to Mr. Farley so they didn't stay. Later Bobby came over and knocked on the door to thank them for the newspaper and the syringe.

"Any progress?" Kim asked him. "Is it okay to ask?"

He grinned. "It's always okay to ask. Not always okay to answer. But since you chaps are my deputies, ex officio, I'll tell you this: the autopsy on William Webb showed traces of cocaine. We're holding Patrick Moon for questioning." He looked at his watch. "Or we were. Nothing to charge him with yet, and by now I guess Haskell has let him go."

"Did you search his house? Patrick's, I mean," Stella asked.

"Yep. Clean as a whistle." He stretched. "Gotta shove off. Take care, you guys." He glanced at the door of the guest house. "There's no lock on this door. You might shove a chair under it, just for the heck of it." He waved and left.

"Was he kidding?" Kim said. "About the door?"

Stella shrugged. "Don't know. If anybody wanted to come for us, they could get in the window easy as pie."

"Boy, that's a thought to go to sleep on." Kim struggled out of her sweat shirt. "I'm going to take a quick swim soon as it gets dark. I'm hot."

One pool light was on, the other out. Those Farleys, Kim thought later as she dove off the board, they could use some new light bulbs. Maybe Patrick swipes them and sells them and palms off old ones on the Farleys. Imagine anybody being dumb enough to hire Patrick Moon and Georgie Foss, the two biggest creeps in town.

She swam fast for several lengths of the pool and then turned over on her back to float for a few minutes. It was a foggy night, and there was a ring around the barely visible full moon. She wondered if Bobby and Haskell would ever find out who killed Bill. When she thought about it, it seemed as if each person she considered was the likeliest suspect. Like an Agatha Christie, with a whole pile of people who had something to hide. Maybe everybody has something to hide.

She turned over again and began to swim, a long, slow sidestroke that her mother had taught her. Her mother said you could tell a person's age by the stroke they used; *her* mother always used the breast stroke, she used the sidestroke, Kim alternated between the crawl and the butterfly most of the time. And what will *my* kids swim like, she wondered. She thought of Alicia wanting to walk on water. If anybody was really high in this bunch, it was Alicia. Her eyes always looked funny.

Without warning she was seized by the shoulders and her head was pushed underwater. She struggled to get free, but the grip of those hands held her. She went limp, thinking she could get loose that way, sliding like an eel out of the fierce grasp, but that didn't work either. The pressure on her chest was building. She could not stay underwater much longer. Her legs kicked out at her attacker, but the person was keeping free of them. With a last effort she tried to get hold of a wrist, to break the hold. Instead, she blacked out.

13

STELLA WAS SO ENGROSSED IN THE HOYLE BOOK, TRY-
ing to understand the equations and diagrams, that
she forgot about Kim. Some unidentifiable sound
made her look up at last, and she realized that the pool
area was very quiet, and that Kim must have been
gone longer than it took for a quick nocturnal swim.

"Kim?" She went outside. The air was heavy with
unspent rain. A sheet of heat lightning lit up the sky
for a moment, but there was no thunder. She walked
to the edge of the pool and looked at the black surface. The one light hardly made a dent in the darkness. Where could Kim be? She wouldn't go anywhere in her wet bathing suit, or without letting
Stella know. A panic seized her, and she tried to calm
down. Her mother always said she was such a wor-
rier. But where *was* Kim?

Dimly she saw the policeman leaning against the
wall at the entrance, looking out toward the road.

He could tell her if Kim had gone out the gate. She started around the pool, heading for him. Kim was a super swimmer, but sometimes people had cramps or something or hit their heads diving.

The underwater lights made the pool a deep blue. Yet as far as she could see nothing seemed to be there that ought not to be. As she reached the shallow end, however, where there were two broad steps under water and one above the waterline, she thought she saw something on the dark upper step. There *was* something . . . or someone. She jumped into the shallow water and approached the steps. Kim was sprawled across the top one, with one leg dangling in the water.

"Kim!" She felt for her pulse. It was beating slowly. Stella yelled for the policeman, and in a minute she heard him come running, while she struggled to lift Kim onto the deck.

Kim gave a strangled little cough; her eyes fluttered open and she stared blankly at Stella.

Phil, the policeman, ran and bent over her. "What happened?"

"I don't know. She went for a swim. I found her on the step there."

"I saw her come out of the cabin. She said she was just going for a quick dip." He lifted Kim. "Let's get her into the cabin. Man, Bobby will have my neck for this."

Stella ran ahead, turned down the blankets on Kim's bed, and got some clean towels. She heard Kim cough again.

Phil brought her in and set her on top of one of the big beach towels. "She's shivering."

"You get out for a minute," Stella said, taking charge. She felt better when she could do something. "I'll get her out of that wet suit and into bed."

"Let me take a look at her head first. Make sure she didn't crack her head. I shoulda looked at it out there. Doc will kill me if I moved her and she's got a concussion."

Kim spoke in a strangled voice. "No. I'm all right." She half sat up suddenly and water rushed out of her mouth. "Ugh. Disgusting." She lay back, exhausted.

Stella got her into bed and threw the wet swim suit into the bathroom. Then she let Phil back in. His broad face was furrowed with worry.

"Make her something hot," he said. "Tea or something. Can you get an outside line on that phone?"

While Stella ran the water out of the tap until it was hot and then poured it over a teabag that she found among the few groceries, Phil called the police office.

It seemed to Stella that Bobby got there in an impossibly short time. He was rather sharp with the penitent Phil and sent him back to stand watch. "And try to keep your eyes open this time." He pulled a chair up beside Kim's bed. "How do you feel? I phoned the doc, but he's out on a baby case."

"I'm all right." Kim was hoarse. "I passed out because I was held under water so long. My throat is sore, that's all. I'm okay."

"Did you see who it was?"

"No."

Bobby tipped the chair back on its hind legs and looked at Stella. "Tell me again just how she was lying there." When Stella had finished, he said to Kim, "Do you think you crawled up on that ledge yourself?"

"No. I was really out of it. Somebody must have put me there."

He lit a cigarette and then said apologetically, "This bother you?"

"No."

It bothered Stella but she didn't want to say so. Smoke gave her hay fever. In a minute she sneezed, and Bobby put out the cigarette.

"It looks," he said, "like somebody wanted to scare you off, not kill you. I guess that's something to be thankful for."

"Small favors," Kim said.

14

PHIL MALONEY SPENT THE NIGHT ON THE FRONT
steps of the guest house. Stella found him there trying
grimly to stay awake when she got up in the morning.
She had looked out to see if they were alone before
she and Kim began to discuss a note that had mys-
teriously appeared in their bathroom overnight. Stuck
through a crack in the window, evidently. She made
a quiet motion to Kim to be still and closed the door.

Soon afterward Bobby and Haskell arrived. They
had called a meeting of the Farley household. Stella
thought Bobby looked tired and strained. Murder was
not something he was accustomed to dealing with.
Even Haskell looked unusually serious and inquired
with concern about Kim's health.

She pulled her hat down to her eyebrows and
scowled. "I'm fine, honest. I hope there's not going

to be a lot of fuss about it. My folks will think I can't look after myself."

"Oh, come on, Kim, no one can look after themselves against a sneak attack like that," Bobby said.

But Stella knew what was bothering Kim, because it bothered her too. Their town had always seemed like such a safe place to live. Probably half the people in town never even locked their doors. Having things happen right here in their midst, things that they thought of as happening far away in cities like New York or Los Angeles or Atlanta, was very frightening. If you couldn't feel safe in your own village, where could you be safe?

They followed Bobby and Haskell up to the house. Phil had been sent home to get some sleep.

"You're going home right after this, right?" Bobby made it a question, but it was an order.

"Sure."

"I've detailed Tommy Kenworth to keep an eye on your house."

"Wow," Stella said. Tommy was very handsome. A year or so ago, she had had a terrific crush on him, though she was too shy ever to say more than "hi" to him. After all, he was an older man. Nearly twenty-five.

As they approached the house, Kim had a sudden attack of nerves. "I guess whoever ducked me will be sitting right there in the living room."

"Maybe you'll know," Stella said. "Like telepathy."

Kim shivered.

"That was a funny report from Charlie Means," Haskell said to Bobby.

"What was it?"

"Said somebody'd raided his garden. Swiped radishes and lettuce, some early peas. He was real mad about the peas; they were some kind of expensive stuff he was experimenting with."

"Raccoons probably," Bobby said.

Haskell pulled a small piece of ragged white denim from his pocket. "Raccoons don't wear jeans."

Stella stared at the cloth. "Or shorts." She looked at Kim.

"David?" Kim said.

"Hasn't that kid turned up yet?" Haskell said. "I didn't think of him."

"I had a couple of the boys search the river," Bobby said.

"No signs?"

"Plenty of signs, but everybody and his brother's down by the river on a good day."

The door opened and Mr. Farley stood there. He looked haggard. "Oh," he said. "It's you folks. Come in, come in." He led them into the living room. "My guests are wondering when you're going to let them leave. They've got things to do at home."

(*114*)

"Soon, I hope," Bobby said. "Will you round them up for us?"

"My wife has a migraine."

"We'll talk to her later then. If you'd get the others, I'd 'preciate it." Bobby wandered around the room after Mr. Farley had gone, examining everything, especially family photographs. "Good-looking boy, that one that died."

"Makes you sick," Haskell said. "Everything to live for."

Alicia came in her housecoat, her face looking drawn. She seemed to have a head cold and was dabbing constantly at her reddened nose with a Kleenex. Stella wondered if she had been crying.

Hank had nicked his chin in shaving. A tiny dried spot of blood remained. Anne looked pale, and she sat by herself, away from the others. The maid and the cook huddled together near the door.

Haskell cleared his throat. "Thank you for coming. Officer Blake has some questions he'd like to ask. He's in charge of this case." He nodded to Bobby.

Bobby was easily the most relaxed person in the room. "I wanted to ask a few questions about last night."

Mr. Farley looked startled. "*Last* night?"

"Yes. Were any of you in the pool area between roughly ten to ten and ten fifteen last night?" He glanced from one to the other. They murmured no, or shook their heads. Alicia blew her nose and said, "Sorry."

"May I ask why you're inquiring about last night?" Mr. Farley was frowning.

They all looked up as Mrs. Farley slid into the room and sat in a chair near the door. She had combed her hair and put on some lipstick, but she looked strained and old. She gave her husband a nervous nod.

"Well," Bobby said, "because that's about the time when somebody tried to drown Kim here."

"Drown!" Mr. Farley said. "Oh, come on, Officer."

The others were staring at Bobby with startled eyes.

"Did any of you hear anything or see anyone out there?"

"I heard her dive in," Anne said. "I heard the splash, and I looked out and saw someone swimming. I couldn't tell who it was."

"Didn't you wonder?"

"Why should I wonder?" Anne said sharply.

"Where were you at the time?"

"I was coming back from a walk."

"Alone?"

"Alone." She thrust her chin out defiantly.

"I see." He made a note. "But you didn't go close to the pool to see who it was."

"I did not."

(*116*)

"I heard it, too." Mrs. Farley's voice sounded thin and high.

"And where were you, ma'am?"

"In the upstairs sitting room. It looks out on the patio."

"And you did not investigate?"

"No."

"Is it usual for someone to go swimming here at night?"

"We have guests," she said vaguely. "I don't interrogate them about their habits."

Mr. Farley was studying Kim. "You look all right, young lady. It *was* you, was it? Or the other one?"

"Me," Kim said. "I'm all right now. Just a sore throat."

"Suppose you tell us what happened, in your own words."

Kim glanced at Bobby, who nodded. "Well, I was hot, and I went out for a quick swim, to cool off. I swam the length of the pool three or four times. Then I was close to the shallow end and somebody grabbed me and ducked me. And held me under."

"Had you heard anyone coming?"

"No."

"Didn't see anyone?"

"No. I was swimming away from the direction of the house, you see."

"Why aren't you dead?" Hank said in a cool, skeptical voice.

"I don't know. I was unconscious. Stell came out to see what had happened to me."

They were looking at her now. Stella said, "I hauled her out, that's all."

"And saw no one?" Mr. Farley was leaning toward them. He seemed to have taken over the meeting from the policemen.

"Nobody at all."

"Very strange. Very strange indeed."

In a sudden loud voice Mrs. Farley said, "What have you men done about finding my boy?"

"Yeah, where is the kid?" Hank asked, in a tone that made Stella and Kim look at him sharply. No one else seemed to notice.

"We've searched the river area quite thoroughly, ma'am," Bobby said. "We found evidence of someone camping out, which happens to be against the law. It might have been your boy."

"I want him found."

"Yes, ma'am. So do we."

"I've looked everywhere I could think of," Mr. Farley said, addressing himself to his wife almost apologetically. "It's not as if he'd made friends yet. I don't believe he knows anybody in town."

"Has he ever run away before?" Stella asked.

"Never," Mrs. Farley said. She took a deep breath.

"I know why he's gone." They all looked at her in surprise. "Yes, I know that much."

"Perhaps you'd tell us, Mrs. Farley," Bobby said.

"He's run away because he thinks I killed Bill Webb."

The room was silent for a moment, and it seemed to crackle with tension.

Mr. Farley said, "Gentlemen, my wife is not well. She has these headaches—"

She interrupted. "I took codeine. The head is not so bad now."

"Why would your son think a thing like that, ma'am?" Bobby said gently.

"Because he saw me turn off the pool lights. The switch is just inside the patio door, and he had come into the room and saw me."

Mr. Farley gave a sharp exclamation. "My dear, you know this isn't true. You must not mislead the police."

"It is quite true." She leaned back and folded her hands.

"Why would you do that?" Bobby asked.

"I wanted them to come inside. I wanted Bill and my husband inside where I could keep track of them, before something happened."

"What did you expect to happen?"

She took a deep breath. There were bright spots of color in her face. "I knew they were talking about my son's death. I knew my husband blamed Bill, and I was afraid of what he might do."

"Amantha!" Mr. Farley sounded shocked.

"He invited our guests in one more attempt to find out what happened to Joshua. He's brooded over it for a year. I was afraid of what he might do."

Everyone in the room was looking at Mr. Farley. His heavy face was white.

After a moment Bobby said very quietly, "Mr. Farley, did you in fact kill Bill Webb?"

Mr. Farley's breathing sounded as if he had been running. "I did not."

"No, he didn't," Mrs. Farley said.

"And how do you know?"

"I would have known if he had. That's all I can tell you."

Haskell spoke. "Did you see who did do it, ma'am?"

"No. It was pitch dark, you know."

Anne spoke. "It was not Bill who was responsible for Josh's death, Mr. Farley."

All the heads swung from Mr. Farley to Anne. She was sitting on the end of her spine, her hands thrust into the pockets of her slacks. She looked truculent.

"Who did, Anne?" Mr. Farley said.

Bobby lifted his hand. "Mr. Farley, I'd appreciate it if you and Miss Putnam would come on down to the office with us. I think we've got a few questions

we'd better get straight before we go any further."
He stood up and glanced at Stella and Kim. "You
kids get your gear, and we'll run you home."

"We've got our bikes," Kim said.

"We'll pick those up later."

Kim and Stella sat in the back seat of the police car,
with Anne, who stared out of the window and never
said a word.

"I hope Nicole sees us," Kim said under her breath
to Stella.

"She'll think we've been arrested."

15

AS SOON AS THEY WERE IN STELLA'S HOUSE, THEY began to talk about the note they had found in the guest house.

> *To whom it may concern, I am alive and well. I have returned to the era of Stonehenge. Do not—* REPEAT *do not—hunt for me. I am invisible to your mortal vision.*
>
> *Yours truly,*
> *David M. Farley.*
> *P.S. Tell my mother I'm okay.*

Sitting in Stella's kitchen they spread the note out on the table and studied it.

"I'd better call Mrs. Farley," Stella said.

"Do you think David might be in danger?" Kim said.

"Who from?"

"Well, I don't know, but he does poke his nose into things. He may know more than is good for him. And I didn't like Hank's tone when he asked about him."

"I'll call Mrs. Farley, and then we'll go look for him."

Mrs. Farley sounded relieved. "When you find him, please tell him he is to come right home. I'm sure he's not eating properly, and he'll catch a cold sleeping down there by the river."

Stella promised to call if they found him. When she hung up, she said, "But I don't know about taking him home. He'd be better off here, till all this mess is cleared up."

"Where do we start to look?"

"Today is the summer solstice. I'll bet he's at his Stonehenge."

It took them a while, without their bikes, to walk down the road to the river. They took the loop that did not pass the Farley house.

"You know, I was thinking," Stella said, "we've been assuming that Georgie and Patrick Moon were peddling dope, just because we know they use it. What if it was the other way around?"

"You mean they were buying from somebody at the Farleys?"

"Yes. Like Hank or Bill or even the girls. A new

Audi is kind of an expensive car for a college kid to be driving, unless his family is loaded."

Thoughtfully Kim said, "It's not. I heard Hank telling Mrs. Farley about his mother. They have a small farm in Ohio or someplace. Some doting relative sent him to Exeter. I guess education is one thing and cars are another in those circumstances." She scuffed up the dust in the road with the toes of her canvas shoes. "But how would Georgie and Patrick know it was available?"

"Patrick hangs around the pool a lot. I've seen him talking to Anne. Supposedly pushing that big thing that cleans the pool. Anyway they say it takes one to know one."

When they were near the river, they walked softly toward the place where David had built his stone circle. Stella, in the lead, put her finger to her lips and pointed. David was sitting with his back toward them, studying his model and eating a banana. His shorts were streaked with mud and his hair was a tangle.

They watched him for a moment, and then Stella said quietly, "Hey, David."

He was on his feet and starting to run, but Kim dived for him and tackled him around the knees. He went down with a thump. She pulled him to his feet, holding onto his arm.

"Sorry, David. I didn't mean to knock you flat.

Don't fight me, don't fight. We aren't going to hurt you."

His face was dirty and tear-streaked. He looked thinner.

"Listen," Stella said, "come on with us to my house. We'll feed you and you can take a shower. You don't have to go home."

"No," he said stubbornly.

"David." Stella's voice was gentle. He was smaller, younger-looking than she remembered him. "Your mom is worried about you. You don't want to worry her when she's got so much else on her mind."

"Is she okay?" His voice was hoarse and anxious.

"Sure. She's fine. Only worried."

Kim said, "She thinks you might have misunderstood, about turning off the lights. You might have thought she was the one that attacked Bill Webb."

Different emotions crossed his face. Finally he said, "Who do they think did?"

"Well, they aren't sure yet, but of course it wasn't your mom. She wouldn't have that much strength. Anyway, she's a kind lady. She wouldn't do a thing like that." In her mind Stella crossed her fingers. She was sure she was right about Mrs. Farley, but she could never prove it. "So why don't you come on home with us, and we'll call her up, or you can, after you've had something to eat."

He hesitated a little longer. "It's not only that. . . ."

he began and stopped himself. The two girls did not pursue it, and finally he went.

"I like your stone cairn," Stella said. "Today is the summer solstice, isn't it."

He looked surprised. "How did you know that?"

"I was reading about Stonehenge."

"How come?"

"Well, I got interested."

He seemed impressed. "I didn't know girls liked that stuff."

Stella laughed, and Kim said, "A male chauvinist in the making."

"I know what that is," he said, "and I'm not." He was beginning to sound more like his old, confident self.

Later, while he was in the shower, Stella brushed some of the dirt from his shorts and shirt and put them in the guest bedroom for him. When he came downstairs, he shone with cleanliness. In short order he had eaten the two big hamburgers Stella had cooked for him, and three glasses of milk. Stella and Kim left him alone in the kitchen so he could phone his mother.

"Tell her we'll bring you home after a while," Stella called back to him. "Tell her when things simmer down." To Kim she said, "I hope she gets the point."

"If she doesn't, we better call her back and make it

clear. I don't think that kid ought to go home now. He knows something."

When they came in again, he was pouring himself some more milk. "My mom's in bed with a headache," he said. "I talked to what's-her-name."

"Which what's-her-name?"

"Alicia. She said maybe she'd come get me after a while." He drank a long swallow of milk, leaving a white moustache on his lip. "Or my sister might come in the MG."

Stella's eyes widened. "Does she have an MG?"

"Yeah. It's an old TD that my dad had fixed up for her. But you wouldn't know what a TD is."

"Listen, Buster," Kim said, "Stella knows more about fancy cars than you'll learn in a lifetime."

"Yeah?" He looked at Stella a moment, then shrugged. "Stonehenge and cars. You're some kind of weird girl." He found an apple and bit into it. "When I get my car, it's going to be the kind that converts to an airplane and a boat when you want it to."

Kim looked at Stella. "Is there such a thing?"

"Not in production."

"I'll have one custom-made," David said loftily.

Kim said, "What you need is a time machine."

"I'm working on it." He opened the refrigerator door. "Is that pudding? Can I have some?"

"It's a week old. I meant to throw it out."

He looked shocked. "Don't do that." He took it, and Stella found him a spoon.

"David, weren't you cold at night?" Kim said.

"I made a neat bed out of pine boughs and stuff."

Stella ruffled his hair. "You're all right, you are." He scowled and pulled away, but he was pleased.

16

TOMMY KENWORTH, LOOKING, STELLA THOUGHT, incredibly handsome in his police uniform, sauntered up the front walk, rang the bell, and poked his head in the door. "Hi, kid," he said in his drawly, slightly mocking voice. "Officer Kenworth at your service."

Flustered, Stella said, "Oh, hi, Tommy. Listen, if it's too hot out there, you can come in—" She broke off and blushed.

Tommy grinned, showing even white teeth. "I'll just settle down on the porch swing, Stell. Bob says you can pick up your bikes at the Town Hall. They're inside. Hey, who's that?"

"This is David Farley. David, this is . . . uh . . . Officer Kenworth."

"Hi," David said. He gave Tommy one encompassing glance and then said, "Can I read your Stonehenge book, Stella?"

"Sure. We'll go get our bikes. Be right back. You stay here, all right?"

But David was already deep in the book.

On the porch, Stella said to Tommy, "I think he ought to stay here till things get settled."

"Sure thing," Tommy said. He put his feet on the porch rail and leaned back in the canvas hammock. "Hey, this is the life." He lit a cigarette.

"We'll be right back."

He waved them off.

At the Town Hall they debated whether it would be all right to ask Bobby if he had found out anything from Anne and Mr. Farley. They went as far as the clerk's desk and asked if Bobby was free.

She looked up from a stack of records. "He took off."

"Where are Anne and Mr. Farley?"

"Gone home, I guess. I think Anne left town." She was obviously busy, so they went back to the front of the building and got their bikes.

Stella was easing hers down the wide steps when she felt a heavy hand grab her shoulder. Startled, she almost dropped the bike, and then turned and saw Georgie Foss grinning at her.

"Don't *do* that," she said.

"Whatsa matter, Stell? Long time no see."

"Like three days," Stella said coldly. "Don't ever grab me like that again."

He gave a high cackle. "Don't like the fellas grabbing you, huh?"

Stella gave him a withering look and went on down the steps.

Kim said, "What are you doing here, Georgie?" She noticed the pupils of his eyes. He was high on something.

"Seein' as how I am a citizen of this town same as you, I guess I got a right. Anyhow I was sent for."

"Who by?"

"Wouldn't you like to know." He tripped on the threshold as he went in and nearly fell.

"Creep," Kim said under her breath.

When they rode up to Stella's front porch, Tommy was reading the *Boston Globe*. He threw his cigarette over the railing, and it made a tiny glowing arc for a moment. "Back already?"

"You want some lemonade, Tommy?" Stella said.

"Sure, if you got any handy."

"I've got some mix. I was going to make some for David."

"The kid? He took off."

Both girls stopped in their tracks.

"Took off where?" Stella said.

"Home, I guess. His mother sent one of those babes that are staying there."

"What car?" Kim said tensely.

"Audi. Real cool job."

Kim and Stella looked at each other.

"We'd better go get him," Kim said.

To Tommy, who was looking puzzled, Stella said, "We think he might have seen things, the night Bill Webb was killed. We were going to tell Bobby he was here, but Bobby's out somewhere."

Tommy looked concerned. "I guess I goofed. You did say to keep him here, but I figured you meant don't let him wander off alone. This babe that came said his mother asked her to pick him up."

"It's okay, Tommy, it wasn't your fault," Stella said, but she was thinking that her former idol was not as bright as he was beautiful. "We'll take a look around. He's probably fine."

"Funny kind of kid." Tommy pushed his hat onto the back of his head. "Asked me if I thought there was human sacrifices at Stonehenge. What the heck is Stonehenge? I've heard the name, but I can't place it."

"Tell you later, Tommy."

The girls wheeled down the road. When they came to the Farley entrance, they stopped and looked down the drive. Bill's car still sat in the semicircle in front of the house, but there was no police car. No one was in sight. The surface of the pool rippled in the breeze.

"Let's go around to the back," Kim said. "We're

going to stick out like two sore thumbs if we go down this drive."

Hank's Audi was still parked in the back. Stella looked at the hood. "He's crazy to leave it under the maple trees. It'll mess up the finish. All that guck that falls off." She pointed to some sap that had fallen onto the hood.

The car was locked. She studied the interior through the window. "Nice car."

"Well, this isn't getting us anywhere. What do we do now? How about if we circle the house, me on the left, you on the right, and meet in front?"

"What will that prove?"

"If David's around, he'll probably pop out of some tree or something. Anyway we can case the joint. If there's nothing in sight, we can just ring the doorbell and ask if we can do anything for Mrs. Farley."

Stella studied the area in back of the house. "I wonder if Mr. Farley came back and if Anne really did go home."

"It would help if we knew what Anne told Bobby."

"Where *is* Bobby anyway?" She started to walk toward the house, then stopped. "Wait a sec."

"What is it?"

"I heard something. Like a hollow thump. Listen! There it is again."

"It's coming from the back of the car."

They turned around and went to the rear of the car.

"It looks as if somebody ran into him," Stella said. "It's sprung." She tried to open it, but it was locked.

The thumping began again. They looked at each other uncertainly.

"Something's in there." Kim tugged again at the unyielding trunk lid.

There was a scraping sound of metal on metal, and a tip of black iron appeared in the crack. Stella jumped back, startled.

"It's a tire iron," Kim said. "Somebody's locked in there." She ran to a pile of brush and stove wood piled up near the garbage cans and grabbed a tough-looking length of wood that was tapered on one end. She got the small end under the narrow opening in the trunk and levered it with all her strength. After a moment of pressure the wood snapped, but it had done its job. The lock sprang open.

Stella seized the trunk lid and pushed it up, then looked inside and gasped.

17

DAVID STARED AT THEM WITH WIDE, FRIGHTENED
eyes. His hands were tied in front of him with
clothesline, and he was gagged. In his bound hands
he held the tire iron. His face was streaked with dirt
and tears.

Stella helped him out, and Kim cut the cord with
her pocket knife and removed the gag. David was
shaking badly.

"What happened?" Stella said. She put her arm
around him.

He leaned against her, and silent sobs shook him.

Kim tensed and stood listening. "I think we'd
better get out of here quick." She shoved down the
trunk lid and led the way, the three of them walking
quickly down the alley, Kim and Stella wheeling the
bikes.

When they had gone a few yards, the sounds Kim

had heard became apparent to Stella and David. Someone was coming from the house toward the alley. Kim ducked into a stand of trees, and Stella and David followed.

Hank came out into the alley. He got into his car and started the engine. They all shrank in their hiding place as he drove past them and down to the end of the alley, where he turned off on the quarter circle that would bring him to the loop road.

David was reluctant to come out of hiding, even after Hank was gone.

"Come on," Stella said gently. "We'll go to my house." She helped David up onto the handlebars of her bike and started for home.

The police car was parked in front of Stella's house, and she was relieved to see Bobby talking to Tommy on the porch. He gave them a quick appraising look and preceded them into the house.

"You guys had me worried," he said. "I thought you were going to stay put."

Stella explained what had happened. Kim meanwhile was heating up some cocoa for David, who still looked frightened. Stella wet a wash cloth at the kitchen sink and gave it to him, while she listened to Bobby. David scrubbed his face hard, as if to obliterate any signs of tears.

"Anne had some interesting stories to tell," Bobby said. "Hey, Kim, can I have some of that cocoa?"

He walked over to the china closet and found a mug. "Apparently nobody intended to kill the Farley boy, but Anne blames Hank because he had supplied the party with acid and PCP and stuff like that, that they most of 'em weren't used to. They were more into reefers and maybe a little coke. It was Hank who laced Joshua's drink. Incidentally Anne said Alicia was in love with Joshua, not Hank, then, though Joshua obviously didn't return the favor." He turned to David. "Davey, do you feel like telling us who trussed you up like a Thanksgiving turkey?"

David said, "Hank."

"Who came to get you?" Kim asked.

"Alicia. She said my mother wanted me. But I never got to go in the house. She drove me around to the alley and left me with Hank. He was waiting. I don't know what he did it for. He never said a word."

Bobby nodded. "According to Anne, Hank and Alicia have got a very profitable little business going, in hard drugs. They're married, by the way."

"Gosh, I never dreamed of that," Stella said.

"Got hitched a while back, mainly so Alicia couldn't be called to testify against him when he was had up on possession charges. Seems Bill didn't approve of what they were doing, and he had said he was going to tell Mr. Farley the whole story about Joshua's death and Hank's little business deals."

"He'll get away," Kim said. "He took off. Hank, I mean."

Bobby nodded. "Tommy saw him go by. I've put out an APB on him."

"Was it Hank that dunked me?" Kim asked.

"I would presume so. Can't prove it. He probably didn't intend to kill you. After all, it's not smart to strew your path with corpses. People get to wondering. I figure he was trying to scare you away from snooping around. Same thing with the message you got. David, did you see anything that might have scared 'em?"

David shrugged. His old self-confidence was coming back. "I see a lot of things."

"Did you see who killed Bill?"

"No." In a more uncertain voice he said, "I thought it was my mom. She turned off the pool light. And then I thought it might be my dad."

"So you ran away."

"Well, I wasn't going to testify that I saw my mom turn out that light, was I?"

"Why did Hank tie you up, David?"

David shrugged again, but Stella had the feeling he was hiding something.

18

"... AND SO," STELLA SAID TO HEN, WHO WAS SIT-
ting in a chair by the hospital room window, looking
pale but interested, "Bobby's put out an All Points
on Hank, David stayed overnight with us and he's
with Bobby now, and that's where today's episode
of *The Perils of Pauline* stands."

"With Pauline hanging on by her fingernails,"
Kim said. They had agreed in advance to make it as
unshocking a story as they could, but Hen was obviously horrified.

"And to think you were right in the middle of it,"
she said. "I feel as if I let your parents down."

"Oh, sure," Kim said, "you should have gone right
on looking after us while your appendix burst. Maybe
we could have gotten you a posthumous Medal of
Honor."

"Which reminds me," Stella said, "I haven't seen Dr. Endicott for a couple of days."

"He's on vacation," Hen said. "He came by to see me before he left. He's on some lake in northern Maine, fishing."

"He'll hate himself for missing all the excitement," Kim said.

Hen looked worriedly at Kim. "You could have been drowned."

Kim laughed. "But I wasn't. Isn't there a poem we learned in elementary school: something like 'The saddest words of tongue or pen are something-something *it might have been!*' "

"Not exactly sad in this case," Stella said.

"So it looks," Hen said, "as if Hank is the all-around villain?"

"Well, I guess so," Stella said. And at that moment something tugged at her mind that she couldn't quite get at. Something she had noticed and half-registered.

The bell rang for the end of visiting hour, and they left Hen with promises to be careful and to pick her up the next morning as soon as she called to say she was ready "to be sprung."

In the afternoon they went back to the Farleys' guest house because Kim had forgotten her toothbrush. Also they were curious to see what was happening, if anything.

No one was in sight, except Georgie, who was

finishing the last section of the wall. Already the house was invisible from the street.

When they reached the pool, Stella noticed that the Roman-striped tents had been taken down. A person would have to change in the house now, if they wanted to swim.

She stood on the circle of trampled grass where one of the tents had been and stared at the other end of the pool, trying to recreate in her mind what she had seen on Sunday before the lights went out. First Mr. Farley and Bill, deep in conversation, standing close to the edge of the pool. Then Hank and Alicia had come out and joined them, Alicia in what looked like Hank's or Bill's T-shirt that was too big for her.

She began recounting aloud. "Alicia tripped over the cord, and Mr. Farley caught her. Mrs. Farley came out, and then Anne. Alicia jiggled on the edge of the pool . . . I suppose she was high, don't you? . . . and Hank grabbed her and said that about walking on water."

Kim took up the narrative. "Mrs. Farley stepped back toward the house, out of the light, and then the light went out."

"Somebody struck a match. There they all were, and then it was dark again. Mr. Farley said that about Patrick not fixing the light."

"And we left the window, and then I thought I heard a splash."

(*141*)

"In the dark, though . . ." Stella wrinkled her forehead in an effort to see the picture in her mind. "Mr. Farley was kind of a pale blob, because he was wearing chinos and a white shirt. And Hank had on khaki shorts and that gray sweatshirt that says DO NOT REMOVE FROM GYM."

"Why do we care what they wore?"

"Because some of them you could vaguely see in the dark. Anne was wearing lemon yellow Bermudas and a yellow blouse. Bill had on jeans and a dark red shirt."

"So?"

"Alicia was in dark clothes, black T-shirt. It seems to me I can remember seeing the vague blur of those light-colored clothes. If somebody in light clothes had stayed close to the pool, wouldn't we have noticed? I thought they had all gone in."

Kim shoved her hat onto the back of her head and pulled thoughtfully on the lock of hair that flopped over her forehead. "The only people in dark clothes were Bill and . . . Alicia? But everybody thinks it was Hank, don't they?"

"I don't know what they think. Maybe he pulled off his shirt so it wouldn't show. . . . No, nobody'd plan that. Well, get your toothbrush and let's split. This place depresses me."

When Kim came back, Stella said, "There's always Patrick Moon."

"He hasn't got brains enough to plan anything."
Out on the road she picked up a flat rock. "That'll
make a good heelstone for David."

"I suppose I have to ask what a heelstone is."

"It's a flat rock that lies on top of two upended
rocks."

"I won't ask why."

"Good, because I can't remember."

19

MR. FARLEY AND HASKELL AMES WERE STANDING IN
the middle of the Farleys' living room talking about
stream fishing in New Hampshire. Mrs. Farley, freshly
made-up and looking calm enough except for the
glint in her eyes, sat by herself on the velvet-uphol-
stered love seat. Jennifer was curled up on the sofa,
reading the *New Yorker*.

After a moment or two, Bobby Blake came into the
room, nodded, looked around.

The quiet of the room was disturbed suddenly by
Alicia's entrance. She looked upset and went directly
to Bobby. "When are you going to let me leave here?"
she demanded. "My friends are gone. Why am I stuck
here?"

He looked at her a moment with a smile. "Miss
Stern, where do you think your friends have gone?"

"God only knows. They didn't even tell me. But that's Anne for you. I did think Hank would have the decency . . ." Her face looked pinched with anger.

"Why don't you take a seat, Miss," Bobby said. "I'd like to bring everybody up-to-date."

Grumbling, she sat down on a straight-backed chair, perched on the edge of it as if to get away as soon as she could.

Stella looked at her and thought of Anne's saying that Alicia had been unrequitedly in love with Joshua. Was she really in love with Hank now? Or had they married just for convenience? Alicia looked unhappy. What a mess it could get to be when people started falling in love. They so often seemed to fall for the wrong ones. Hormones ought to be kept on a shelf where you could take them down when you really needed them, not have to bother with them when you didn't want to.

Bobby looked at Haskell. "I don't think we need to bother the ladies in the kitchen."

Stella smiled to herself. Who but Bobby would think of calling them "the ladies in the kitchen." The phrase identified them and managed not to put them in a category.

Haskell nodded and cleared his throat. "Officer Blake and I have made some progress since we saw you last."

"Good," Mr. Farley said heartily. Jennifer looked

up from her book and shot a glance of annoyance at her father.

"Thanks to quick action on the part of Stella and Kim here, another possible tragedy was prevented." Briefly he described their discovery of David, and Hank's departure. The astonishment on his listeners' faces certainly looked real, Stella thought.

"You mean *Hank* was . . . was kidnapping that kid?" Alicia said in a faint voice. She stared at Stella and Kim. "You made it up."

"Oh, no," Bobby said. "They didn't." He went to the door. "David, come here, please." David came in, looking self-conscious and swaggering a little.

"David, describe please what happened."

David told them, obviously enjoying the drama.

Mrs. Farley spoke for the first time. "I don't understand what you and David are saying, Officer."

Bobby said it again, patiently.

"But why would Hank do such a thing?"

"Perhaps he'll tell us when he gets here."

Stella looked at Bobby quickly. Had they really caught him?

He noticed her glance and nodded. "Tommy picked him up in Lynnfield. We had a call from a state trooper who stopped him for speeding."

"What are you charging him with, Officer?" Mr. Farley asked. He looked pale and tense.

"Assault and intent to kidnap, for one thing," Bobby said. "And possession."

"Of what?"

"Drugs," David said. "A whole bunch. Powdered stuff. Different kinds, I think. I found it." He looked pleased with himself.

"Found it where?" his father said.

"In a trick compartment in his briefcase. All done up nice and neat in glassine envelopes. I wasn't sure what it was, but I knew it had to be some kind of dope. Why else would Patrick Moon and Mr. Foss be buying it from him?"

"And what were you doing in Hank's briefcase?" Jennifer said. It was the first time Stella had seen her look interested in anything.

For a moment David was disconcerted. Then summoning up his poise he said, "It was my duty to check out Hank and Bill. They were practically strangers, after all. They might have come here to kill us."

"You're preposterous," Jennifer said. "Mother, you really ought to—" She broke off at the look on her mother's face. "What is it, Mom?"

"What did you do with the drugs, David?" Mrs. Farley said.

"I hid it under the Altar Stone at Stonehenge."

"David," his father said sharply, "answer your mother."

"But I did, Dad. It isn't there now because I gave it to Officer Blake."

Mrs. Farley slumped back in her chair, with a look of despair.

Bobby had been watching her closely. "Did . . . er . . . did Hank ever persuade you to try his product, Mrs. Farley?"

Mr. Farley answered, his face growing red. "Look here, Blake, I won't have you insulting my wife."

Haskell Ames put his hand on Mr. Farley's arm. "We have to ask questions, Mr. Farley. No insult intended."

Mrs. Farley spoke directly to her husband when she answered. "I tried it, yes. Hank thought it would help my nerves."

Mr. Farley gave a muffled exclamation and buried his face in his hands.

"And it did, you know." Mrs. Farley looked brighter for a moment. "I felt as though I could see the reasons for everything, understood everything, even Joshua's death."

"Mom," Jennifer said, and began to cry silently.

"We know," Bobby said, looking uncomfortable at all the emotion he had unleashed in the room, "that Bill Webb disapproved of Hank's being a supplier and was trying to stop him. We have no proof yet, but we expect to learn eventually that Hank was anxious to silence Bill, to protect his drug trade. Hank has been cleaning up. In fact he had decided not to go back to college next year. He and Alicia were going to set themselves up in the drug racket on an even bigger scale."

"You'll never pin the murder on Hank," Alicia said. "He's too smart for you."

"And you were one of his best customers, weren't you, Miss Stern," Bobby said. "It must be a bit rough on you now that he's gone and you can't get your hands on any dope. Makes you jumpy, I should imagine."

With an effort Alicia stayed calm. "You squares think everybody who dabbles a little in drugs is a junkie. It's no different from having a couple of drinks."

"That's an argument I run into quite a lot," Haskell Ames said in his pleasant conversational voice. "There really are a couple of differences though. One: dope is often addictive. And two: it's illegal."

Alicia sneered at him. "Drinking isn't addictive?"

"Not unless the person is an alcoholic. Normal people can take it or leave it."

"You small town cops make me laugh," Alicia said. "Always the homespun philosophy. What do you know about anything?"

"It's true we aren't as sophisticated as New York

cops," Bobby said, "but we muddle through." He gave her a friendly grin. "One thing we haven't figured out though is why did you kill Bill Webb?"

For a moment there was not a sound in the room. Then Alicia jumped to her feet, shouting a long list of obscenities, some of which Stella realized she had never even heard before. Alicia ended by saying, "You think you can trap an innocent person. Well, you can't."

Bobby looked at Stella. "Stell, tell us again just what you saw before the pool lights went out, and afterward."

Stella felt like hugging him. She knew now that he had picked up on her information about what they were all wearing and had seen its significance long before she did. Trying hard to keep her voice steady, she retold what she had seen.

"Thanks, Stell. You see, folks, there were only two people in that group who would have been just about invisible in the dark. The two people who were wearing dark clothes. Bill Webb in his jeans and dark shirt, and Alicia in her black T-shirt."

Alicia's face was distorted. "You're insane!" She ran for the door and almost made it, but Kim stuck out her foot and tripped her. Haskell Ames picked her up. Alicia was sobbing now.

"He was going to ruin everything," she said. "He'd have gotten Hank arrested and sent up. The business would be gone. My source would have been gone. And he was going to tell Mr. Farley it was Hank's acid that killed Joshua. . . ."

"He had already told me," Mr. Farley said grimly. "I reported it to Officer Blake."

". . . and for a while," Bobby said ruefully, "Officer Blake lit on the wrong suspect."

"I thought my mother did it," David said.

"Oh, David." She gave him a beseeching look. "I thought it was your father."

"Mr. Will Shakespeare is not the only one who can make up a comedy of errors," Haskell said. "Let's get this young lady down to headquarters, Bobby. Our thanks to all of you for your help." He reached out and patted Stella's arm. "Special thanks to you two girls. We're all indebted to you."

"Except Alicia," David said.

20

STELLA AND KIM SAT ON THE FLOOR BESIDE THE SOFA where Hen was stretched out. They had finished telling her all the parts of the story that she had not heard before, and she was still amazed.

"I had a postcard from Mom today," Stella said. "She said they were having a wonderful time, and she hoped everything was going smoothly here." She grinned. "Wait'll she hears. One woman being tried for murder, one man charged with assault, attempted kidnap, and running a dope trade. One woman just barely escaping getting turned on to drugs for good. One kid almost kidnapped. Patrick Moon and Georgie Foss charged with possession of hard drugs."

Hen shook her head. "What you two get up to when I look the other way."

"Oh yes," Kim added, "one appendix missing."

The phone rang, and Stella answered it. She came

back looking pleased. "That was Jennifer with a message from her folks. We get to use the tennis court and the pool any time we want."

"Hallelujah," Kim said. "Nicole can keep her old country club courts."

"Oh, I forgot to tell you," Hen said, "Nicole is coming over this afternoon."

Stella and Kim groaned. Life was back to normal.